# BEST
# WOMEN'S EROTICA
# OF THE YEAR

### VOLUME ONE

# BEST
# WOMEN'S EROTICA
# OF THE YEAR

## VOLUME ONE

*Edited by*
RACHEL KRAMER BUSSEL

CLEiS
PRESS

Published in the United States by Cleis Press, an imprint of Start Midnight LLC, 101 Hudson Street, 37th Floor, Suite 3705, Jersey City, New Jersey 07302.

Printed in the United States.
Cover Design by Scott Idleman/Bink
Cover photograph: iStock
Text design: Frank Wiedemann
First Edition.
10 9 8 7 6 5 4 3 2 1

Trade paper ISBN: 978-1-62778-153-4
E-book ISBN: 978-1-62778-159-6

Library of Congress Catalog-in-Publication Data is available on file.

# CONTENTS

# INTRODUCTION

It's an incredible honor to present to you *Best Women's Erotica of the Year Volume 1*, my first time taking the helm. As an author, this groundbreaking series has been home to some of my favorite stories I've written, stories that pushed me into uncharted territory, whether writing about a dishwashing fetish ("Doing the Dishes"), an oral sex restaurant ("Secret Service") or visiting a married lover ("Espionage").

As an editor, I faced the mighty task of whittling down the over two hundred submissions I received to the twenty-two found between these covers. The resulting collection is one that features the kind of women I consider my readers to be: smart, daring, fierce, loving, kinky, curious, powerful, feisty. While no single book can represent every kind of woman, you'll find women from a range of races, sexual orientations, and backgrounds, partnered and solo. You'll find women going on sexual journeys from the past, present and future.

Whether they're enjoying a threesome, acting out their passion on stage, getting a tattoo, seducing their boss, having their naked body painted, dressing up as a domme or exulting in their most submissive moment, the characters you'll read about here, and their authors, are passionate, funny and they were a delight to visit with.

You will notice that there are more than a few women here "of a certain age," as the saying goes, which is fitting as I turned forty just before this book goes to press—close enough to look back on my younger days, as Aya does in "Revisiting Youth" by J. Crichton and H. Keyes, and hoping to keep the erotic spark alive well into the future, as characters like D in Dorothy Freed's "Two Doms for Dinner" do.

My goal with this book was twofold: to present sexual fantasies in a way that sparks your imagination and also respects your mind, and to reflect a glimmer of real life back from the deepest reaches of these authors' minds. Though some of the scenarios you're about to read would be impossible to live out, and some might be unlikely, all of them offer women who are willing to go toward what might seem scary or new or uncertain, whether that means an old flame, a sexy stranger or a childhood crush.

I also wanted to present some of my favorite erotic authors, such as S.E.C.R.E.T. trilogy author L. Marie Adeline and The Original Sinners series author Tiffany Reisz, alongside writers whose work you may be reading for the first time. I've long said that erotica is an incredibly democratic and welcoming genre, and I'm proud to have so many new authors, whose names you'll likely want to watch as they set forth in their erotica writing careers.

Whether outdoors, in a love hotel or even a porta-potty (yes, you read that right, and Amy Butcher's "Waiting to Pee" is one of the most provocative stories I've ever published, one I plan to reread often), they are willing to go forth into the unknown because the payoff promises to rock their worlds. I hope the same can be said for your reading experience. Welcome to Best

Women's Erotica. Whenever and wherever you're reading this, I hope it both arouses and surprises you.

Rachel Kramer Bussel
Atlantic City, New Jersey

# A NEW CANVAS

by Tara Betts

The bass and slow pace of hip hop sounded like a drone after a couple of hours. Everything sounded as if it had the same pace then. When the dark room was even more obscured by smoke from blunts and a twinge of incense, Angela spotted Troy. She hadn't been smoking and neither had he. For both of them, it was about being in the same space with the artists and loving the music. They would meet for dinner sometimes, talk politics, books, music and all that, but there was never a flirtation. Usually, Angela had a boyfriend or Troy had a girlfriend, and Angela simply kept quiet about how she felt about Troy listening intently to her every answer, her glimpses of one of his dozen tattoos, the lingering conversations where it took forever for Angela to get out of the car, their long goodbye hugs and even how his posture made him look strong, confident and sexy. Sexy. She could not even say the word out loud. She had not dated anyone seriously in almost three years.

She wanted him, but Angela was afraid to lose the amazing

conversations, so she kept it at just friends. She tried not to think about how the steady thump of the bass reminded her of the pulse of her clit, and she quieted herself. She avoided looking at his lower lip like she wanted to suck it gently, or at the piercings on his ear; her tongue could almost taste each of the metal studs. Snap out of it. That lingering was gone in a blink, and he was doing a frenetic bounce, making fun of someone's dance he saw the other night. He could break her into giggling too fast, but he seemed to like making her laugh, so she went with it. It was already late when they saw each other at The Spot, and the ongoing thump was starting to sound gloomy and indistinct, so she said she was leaving. "I can give you a ride back to the crib," he said. It didn't seem like anything he'd never offered before. She said yes.

Her discomfort lingered the most when they could never just say goodbye in his car. They always ended up talking in the car and staring at her door, as if he wanted to stay in the car or follow her. Finally, after sitting in the car for the longest pause, she piped up and said what she had always wanted to say. "It's not too late if you want to come in. I was going to make some tea and maybe watch a movie." Even this felt too forward to her, but his hands relaxed on the steering wheel.

"Sure, let me grab my bag. There's something I've been working on," Troy said.

He leaned over the back seat and pulled out a half-zipped backpack. Angela thought it was a laptop until she spied the hardcover journal, Sharpies, markers, pens and colored pencils. She hadn't seen those in years, but she knew what they were right away. She was so excited that she could almost smell Krylon. Troy, who hadn't done graffiti in years, still sketched in a piece book. Usually it was the small-scale version of what ended up on brick walls or commissioned murals, but this was his private haven of characters, panels, miniature versions of letters rendered in bubbled curves and wild-style angles.

"I'd love to see what you're drawing. I didn't know you got down like that!" Angela said.

She was surprised and intrigued that she saw this creative side in him. She figured he was always about his work, but this was new. She wished she could draw him nude, then snapped back to attention before she started feeling too overheated and wet from the thought of him touching her.

"I thought it would be cool to share something with you," he said.

"I'd like that," Angela said. She hopped out of the passenger's side and waved him toward the vestibule. "What have you been working on?" she asked.

"A lot of random sketches, but there has been a series on my mind, and it makes me wish I could paint it on trains and go all-city!"

"You know no one does that anymore, but the idea of doing a throwback like that is nice. Too bad they shrink-wrap the trains in those ugly advertisements instead," Angela said.

"Right? Those kinds of pieces are something you see in old movies, but the series just struck me as that kind of classic," Troy said.

"Now I'm curious. I have ginger peach, green tea and honey chamomile. What kind do you want?" Angela asked. She was putting a full kettle on the stove. She liked to hear the building rumble and the eventual prelude to the whistle. She turned around to reach for the closed box of tea and realized he was standing in the doorway, quietly watching her.

"Ginger peach," Troy said.

"Show me the piece book already!" Angela said, her tone partial command, but more gentle curiosity.

"You sure you want to see it?" he asked.

"Yes!" Angela said. For the first time ever, he hesitated, and then she started to wonder. Some of the landscapes were city scenes—brick walls with kids leaning against them, trains snaking above the dark streets dotted with a few lights, letters spelling out names of crews. Then there was one sketch with butterflies and intricate letters that stopped her from reaching for a second cup of honey chamomile. It spelled out her name in orange and yellow with twinges of red. It reminded her of the sun at dusk. "Troy, this is beautiful..." Angela was cut off before she could say anything else.

He cupped his hand in the small of her back, and pulled her close. She was stunned that it was actually happening, but leaned a little bit forward. He nipped at her bottom lip, and when the first full kiss came, her tongue pressed past his lips and twisted toward his tongue. She was trying to slow down, but he was holding her. She had dropped the piece book on the table, and grabbed his head by then. The only thing that broke her focus was the hard whistle of the kettle. She stumbled a few steps away, but he would not let go of her hand. He looked so serious that heaven breaking in fragments and raining down on them was not going to change his intentions.

"I actually wanted to suggest something..." Troy said.

The deliberation let her know that this might be more than she expected, but she only asked, "What?"

"Well, I had these pens that I wanted to try on a new canvas," he said. He was trailing off again, but a small smirk crossed his mouth. "I was wondering if you'd want to take off your clothes and let me draw on you."

He had found a set of body art pens. They reminded Angela of eyeliner pencils, soft but in more colors than she'd seen at the cosmetic counters. He took out the purple one. "Your favorite color," Troy said as he took the pen and ran the slender, covered tip behind her ear, stopping at her collarbone. She kissed him again, and gently grabbed his earlobe between her teeth.

"Only if you end up naked too," Angela said. She found herself wondering who the woman in her body was. She started by taking off his T-shirt and watching his locks fall across his lean chest and broad shoulders. Dear Jesus, even that much skin, plus seeing the other tattoos that she had never seen, took her breath away. His skin was covered with poems and Adinkra symbols.

Angela unzipped her hoodie and revealed the tank top underneath. Her nipples visibly hardened, as if they were defying her bra. He leaned in, kissed her and deliberated at her collarbone while he unbuttoned her jeans. He studied her face intently before licking the hollow of her collarbone and cupping her left breast. When she bent a bit to lower her pants, he eased the tank top over her head. When the pants fell, he grabbed her close and said, "This is going to go slow, just like teasing the rest of you."

Angela's mouth fell open. She was still stunned that her tea kettle might not be the only vessel making a high-pitched sound. Troy asked her to grab a blanket and a couple of pillows that he could spread on the floor. Angela, half-naked, obliged.

When she came back, Troy was standing in her kitchen looking like all the lean muscle that she had imagined in his baggy jeans and Timberland boots. He was already half erect and leaning to the left. She was trying not to stare. He had more to offer than she'd imagined. She had known him all this time, but just him touching her and finally meeting her mouth with his had broken her defenses. He smoothed out the blanket on the kitchen floor and took one of the pillows from her.

She felt a bit awkward, but he asked her to lay on her stomach at first. Before a pen touched her skin, he rubbed her shoulders, then pressed his fingertips down and ran them along the length of her back. She felt his lips kiss each vertebrae in her spine until he reached the curve of her ass. "Turn over," he said. Troy took in the length of Angela's body and traced his tongue between her breasts, then grabbed the right one. He teased the nipple with his tongue until it puckered into hardness. His warm breath and his coppery locks brushed against her bare skin. When she felt a pulse quickening at the tip of her clit, a small moan escaped her lips. He spread out the rest of the body art pens near the blanket. "Just relax and be still," Troy said. Angela didn't know if she could stand it, but she was curious to see what he would sketch on her.

At first, the cool, firm tip of each pen chilled her skin. She felt the goosebumps rise as he wrote *Uhuru*, the Swahili word for freedom, on her left forearm. He colored in the purple letters with pink and blue chevron-like stripes. He moved on to the right forearm and wrote *if*, the Yoruba word for love, in black. He colored in that shorter word with red and green. On the left side, he started drawing a purple arrow along the length of her body toward the pubic bone. "Directions for later," Troy explained. When he was done drawing that arrow, he capped the pen and traced the tip around the lips of her opening, which had been wet when he began. He stroked her clitoris a few times with the pen and Angela shuddered. When he touched her with his fingers, he smiled, reached for the black pen and drew the second arrow between her breasts, right next to the purple one.

Just above the collarbone, he etched in a purple and navy skyline, but included an array of tiny gold stars across her hips. A few outlined the constellation Cassiopeia between her shoulder and breast. When he got to her thighs, he started to sketch out anatomical images of the brain and the heart on one side and the uterus and tongue on the other. He leaned over and kissed her, and told her that her eyes and lips always drew him in, but the brain and the heart made it better. He loved how every word fell from her tongue, and he wondered what her babies might be like inside her. He drew monarch butterflies trailing up one leg and toward her inner thigh. It almost looked like the migration to Michoacán had landed on her leg. On her other leg, there were blackbirds in midflight. Their wings were tipped in bright green and silver.

As the ink dried, his lips worked their way back up her legs. She felt him inhale and exhale over the soft curls that covered her outer lips. He was breathing in her smell.

"I have to know what you taste like," Troy said.

He gently lifted her legs a couple of inches. He had not even parted them yet, but she said yes anyway. He spread her legs and let them rest on his shoulders. She wanted to know what he spelled out on the button of flesh, and he seemed to lap up her wet quivering. Angela looked down to see him drinking her in while her decorated legs were in full sight. She felt his soft skin covered in tattoos, and the muscles pressed into her soft flesh; that alone made her moan more and grab fistfuls of the blankets in both hands.

"Are you ready?" Troy asked. Angela nodded. When he started to ease his way into her, she felt like her body could not remember this first thrust ever feeling so full, tight and electrifying all at once. She clutched his lower back and felt him move even faster, but not too fast. He listened to her breathing and synced his breath with hers. They clutched each other's hands and Angela rose her hips to meet his. She got louder. Troy said, "Damn, girl, it's like that?" A small smile parted Angela's lips.

"Yeah, it's like that." She felt the familiar tightening of a man's legs and saw Troy's eyes clench before he asked her to slow down.

They waited for a few breaths before he flipped her on top of him in a quick, confident motion. It reminded her of how comfortable he was just standing in front of a room full of people, and how she found that sexy—but now she wanted to scream, though she knew she was not quite there. She was on top of him now and leaning forward. She wondered what all his designs looked like on her body from this angle, but she was leaning into him to feel all his heat, his skin. He pulled back just enough to almost be free then plunged inward to enter her even deeper. She leaned down with her elbows on either side of his head and grabbed his face to kiss him so hard that she could almost feel his teeth. She nipped at his lip.

They started moving faster, and she guided him into a steady, rhythmic pace, where she felt the orgasm growing like the quick moment when a sparkler ignites and then blooms into bright sparks. Shuddering, she said his name. She gripped the shaft even tighter while he began flexing inside her. It felt like a second pulse beating hard and fast, and soon Angela was yelling "Don't stop." They were clamped onto each other so tightly that she didn't even notice how loud they both were until she collapsed and rested her head on his chest.

"You loud as hell, girl," Troy said. He was smirking now. Angela hit him with a pillow.

"I can be loud again. What you gonna do about it?" They giggled softly.

"Just let me know when you need me to be a canvas again," Angela said.

# DEMIMONDE

## by Valerie Alexander

On the night of the séance, my cousin Ora lays on my bedroom chaise and tells me that we are about to be visited from beyond the grave. "They say Celeste Clair saw her dead mother appear right there in the dark—and Miss Greenbow was told she'd marry by summer."

I wind my long black hair into a rope and pin it up. "You'll be told of your future husband too. These traveling mediums deal in flim-flam, Ora. Pure nonsense."

Ora sits up, indignant. "Elizabeth! Why are we going to the spirit parlor tonight if you're going to be gloomy?"

I check my reflection in the looking glass. The séance will be held at Lady Wentworth's, and all of her Fifth Avenue friends will be there; it's important my deep-blue evening dress with the open neckline is respectable for a widow of thirty-one. "How else am I to amuse myself?"

Down the oak staircase we go, electric lights burning dimly from hallway sconces. The house is quiet, my infirm mother-in-law asleep upstairs for the night. The butler opens the heavy front door to a snowy 72nd Street.

"Mother says these table-tappers are a wicked blasphemy," Ora says happily as we climb into the hansom. "She will be so livid that we've gone."

My cousin is quivering with excitement; at twenty-four, she rarely goes out unescorted at night. Despite it being 1899 and New York perched on the edge of a new century, my aunt is terribly strict about Ora's freedoms. A member of the temperance movement, she is scandalized when we ride bicycles in Riverside Park and frowns on my uncle's cognac and cigars. She is desperate for Ora to marry soon, and considers me a bad example for refusing to remarry in the six years since my husband's death.

Like everyone else, she thinks I'm waiting for a wealthy railroad magnate, maybe, or a banker from an old family. Or, possibly, that I'm waiting for my sweet bedridden mother-in-law to pass on before I choose a new husband to replace her son. It never occurs to anyone that I'm waiting for passion. But I know I could meet someone; I could meet the devil himself, handsome and tall, with a beautiful mouth like the doorway to the doom where all fallen women go.

Fallen women. It's the worst fate that can happen to women like Ora and me, but the idea of the falling itself sounds like a swoon in a dream.

I could meet someone like that. I could meet him tonight.

Off we go in the hansom. Snow is falling past the gas lamps. Ora reminds me that tonight's medium, Madame Morgana, is known throughout Europe. "She is not like those soothsayers in the Bowery. Real spirits will appear to us!"

The carriage stops in front of the Wentworths' Fifth Avenue mansion. Upon entering I see the Wentworths' drawing room has been transformed into a proper spirit parlor with long, plum-colored drapes hanging from the walls, and creamy tapers flickering in the candelabras. Eight women and three bewhiskered older gentlemen surround a circular table. The hearth is unlit, I notice. How odd on a January night.

"Ladies, gentlemen."

He enters. Twenty-five years or so, with longish brown hair and a smile that is like the sun rising over the trees. So handsome yet so innocent he looks, as if unaware of his charm. Which is how I know he's a rake.

"I am Theobald Moore," he says. "Your master of ceremonies tonight while we await Madame Morgana."

Clearly he is the lure to bring in the ladies. His beautiful smile, his animal vitality, are the only sparks of life in this sepulchral room.

Ora is fairly wriggling in her seat. Theo kisses her hand. He asks who she would like to hear from and she mentions a former teacher from her finishing school. Then his hazel eyes connect with mine. I forbid myself to smile but I can't help it, and he laughs.

"I had a feeling you and I would meet," he says, taking my hand. A true dandy, he smells faintly of bergamot and lavender. "I had a vision of a young raven-haired beauty who would grace our séance."

Some of the women look quite impressed with this. But Lady Wentworth sniffs; she's disliked me since I spurned the hand of her nephew several years ago.

"And who have you lost, Miss…?"

"Mrs. Pond. I am here only for my cousin."

"Elizabeth has lost her husband," Ora says, for she can never be quiet. "Six years now."

"A widow," he says. "Six years. Such a *long* time." And though he looks suitably sympathetic, his eyes hold mine in a way that says he understands just how long I've been waiting— and what I've been waiting for.

Madame Morgana sweeps into the room. She's dressed primly in black calico and a lace collar fasted by an ivory brooch, but her pale eyes regard us disdainfully.

"My dear friends," she begins. "Tonight is a celebration of the gifts of the sages of the ages. Clairvoyance, crystal-gazing, mesmerism, chiromancy and above all, spiritualism. I was born with the ability to communicate with departed souls. Today, trained by the masters of alchemy, divination and magic, I will humbly serve as your conduit to your loved ones in the beyond."

I glance at Theobald. He smiles winsomely.

"Now I must ask you to place both hands on the table," Madame Morgana says.

An array of hands circle the velvet-covered table—veined, smooth, puffy, jeweled—just before Theo extinguishes the flames. The drawing room is plunged into blackness.

Ora's hand gropes for mine in the eerie atmosphere. "Something brushed the back of my neck!" gasps Mrs. Rutledge. A moment later another woman cries, "It touched my hand!" There does seem to be a chill in the drawing room, but is it a ghostly presence or simply a cold room with no fire?

Something trails across my shoulder. But these aren't the ephemeral hands of a spirit. These fingers are hot and dry and purposeful as they stroke my neck.

A shivery thrill shoots through me.

Theo's fingers gently circle my ears. An odd thing, but it awakens my nerves and reminds me that I have not been touched by a man in years. Next his hands slide down my throat and over my collarbone. There they hesitate, perhaps waiting for my protest, but at my silence, his fingertips continue their descent into my décolletage.

My face flames, yet I arch my back, signaling him to continue. Inside the velvet bodice of my dress his fingers go. Into my corset and chemise until he cups my breasts. My skin prickles with heat. I can't be allowing this, a stranger touching me in a dark room even as I'm surrounded by matrons who could ruin me.

His mouth brushes my neck. He rolls my nipples back and

forth until they're stiff, then pulls on them lightly. I begin to shake.

"Spirit, if you are here, speak to us!" Madame Morgana cries.

My petticoats rustle as his hands move lower.

Madame Morgana says again, warningly, "Spirit, are you here?"

The hands withdraw. An odd moan fills the other end of the room, followed by a rustle, and a small, veiled white form moves into the room. Ora squeezes my hand as the spectral figure moves closer, almost glowing in the dark.

"Spirit" speaks in a feminine, childlike voice, with predictions for us all. Various loved ones send wishes from the beyond. Ora will marry a rich gentleman from Chicago. And me, well, I am going to go on a great adventure in a world that is both nearby and faraway.

The drawing room lights come on to reveal tear-streaked faces. One of the older women looks disgruntled and mentions pointedly that the medium she saw in London emitted real ectoplasm. But Ora is thrilled. "I told you it was real!" she whispers.

As we bid Lady Wentworth good-bye, my cheeks burn at the thought of the liberties I just allowed Theo. But he meets us at the door and reminds me that he is available for private ghostly sessions should I care to call on him.

"I admire your talent," I manage to say, avoiding his eyes, "but I am very occupied with my charity work."

"I have more talents than you saw tonight."

How brash. But in the carriage going home, I can't forget his hands sliding into my bodice, his mouth on my throat. I would have permitted him anything. How close I came to disgrace.

In my salon the next day, I stare at the flames in the fireplace. I've cranked the phonograph to play a Brahms concerto, and a novel is abandoned on my lap. It's my usual life of books and music here in this room of forest-green wallpaper and somber oil paintings. But I can't help ruminating over Theo: a penniless youngest son, maybe, getting through the world on his wits and his smile.

The clatter of hooves just outside. My body tenses. But it couldn't be him, unless Lady Wentworth has provided my address.

The butler announces him. "Theobald Moore."

That beautiful grin ignites my salon. "Mrs. Pond."

I cannot repress my smile. How impudent. How bold. I shouldn't be charmed, but I am.

"You seemed distressed last night," he begins. "I felt I must come here today to offer my services—should you require them."

In this quiet cocoon, he seems to crackle with life, brighter than the fire.

"How generous. What services would those be?"

He brings out a velvet pouch. "I will read your fortune," he says, handing me a large deck of hand-painted tarot cards. "Shuffle the cards and we will see what destiny has in store for you."

I choose three cards: the Knight of Wands, the Two of Cups and the Star. "An intoxicating union," he says. "Not a lasting love, but a fleeting and exciting adventure."

At least he's honest.

"Perhaps yours will happen tonight," he says. "I am attending a masked party."

A strange heat creeps up my spine. He is not speaking of a respectable event, I know it. "Lady Wentworth again?"

"No. This is near Madison Square, at the home of a woman you may not know." My trepidation must show on my face for he adds, "Everyone will be masked—no one will know who you are. So, you see, it will be an adventure."

I feel faint with dread and excitement as I agree to go.

That night the hansom arrives at nine o'clock. I take a shot of sweet apricot brandy to settle my nerves, then tell my butler I must check on a friend who's taken ill. He doesn't believe me, of course. It is too unusual, a beautiful young man calling on me in the afternoon and an outing late that night. But as soon as the carriage door closes, I see the dark-blue mask on the opposite seat and I smile.

The driver takes me to Madison Square. Shadows move under the gas lamps, through the pools of golden light on the snowy walks. This is the New York night world I so rarely see.

The carriage stops in front of a brownstone. A man is waiting outside; his brilliant smile identifies Theo immediately under his black mask. "You did come. I love a woman of courage."

We enter the house. Last year Ora had gotten hold of a New York guidebook which described saloons in thrilling detail, even ones with rouged and powdered male performers; several saloons were reputed to have basement brothels. Yet as Theo takes me into a foyer of stuffed wild animals and high ceilings, I know this night will be far more exotic and disgraceful. Two masked women lead us into a room of damask and gilt couches, while a masked man serves us red wine. Several musicians play the violin and cello in the corner.

I feel as if I am in an opium dream. This is the demimonde, disreputable people drinking and playing games in states of undress. My rose-colored dress seems mortifyingly modest.

At the front of the massive room a shirtless man with black, curly hair claps his hands. "It's time for the game," he announces. "All players must assemble here by the fire."

I look questioningly at Theo. "A game of yes and no," he says. "You will see."

He joins eight other men and women by an enormous piano. The black-haired man says, "Begin. Who am I thinking of?"

"Myself and Gertie!" calls out one of the white-robed women. "No."

The woman removes her robe. She is wearing only cotton

pantaloons underneath, no chemise. I almost choke, shocked by the sight of a bare-breasted woman standing so confidently before so many men.

"Charlotte and Douglas," suggests Theo.

"No."

Theo removes his shirt, exposing a broad, smooth chest. Another woman guesses incorrectly and undresses down to her lace shimmy; she is quite small, and her familiar voice tells me that she played the role of "Spirit" last night at the séance. At last someone guesses correctly by naming Gertie and Bridget, which forces the black-haired man to remove his trousers. The participants then begin guessing physical acts, some of which I have never heard. "Doing the dog." "Quim on quim." At last a woman cries out, "Bridget fucking Gertie with a candle!" and the man concedes her victory.

"Strip!" she commands. I watch with a shocked and thumping heart as the black-haired man steps out of his undergarments, revealing his hard, thick cock to the room.

My face burns with heat. I will never survive the scandal if I am unmasked. But a flame of lust is flickering inside me, and my head swims with the delirious awareness of my evaporating control.

"I'm bored," the man announces. He leans one elbow on the piano as he sips his wine, still naked. "Theo, entertain us with your mind-reading game."

They dim the electric lights so there's just the firelight. Theo closes his eyes. "One mind burns brighter than the rest," he says after a moment. "A woman's mind. A woman who dreams every night of her unlived life."

My skin prickles. But of course whatever he says will be a trick.

"You think of when you were nineteen, when you let a young man feel under your dress in your aunt's summer house in the country. And sometimes you pretend another gentleman has taken you over his lap to spank you like a maid who's spilled the tea."

All the masked faces are watching me, not Theo. They know it's me he's speaking of.

"Sometimes you dream of a man tied to your bed, naked and blindfolded for you to use as you please. Other times you want to be dressed in trousers and a waistcoat while a man buggers you like a boy."

My cunt is tingling, the tops of my thighs wet.

"...And last night, after you let me touch you, you wished all the way home in the carriage that I was fucking you."

I swiftly exit the room, the brownstone, startling the hansom driver who's fixing the horse's bridle and blanket. Theo follows.

"Elizabeth, please wait."

He gives the driver some money and a brief instruction, then climbs into the carriage after me. Off we go. The hansom is cold and snowflakes cling to the windows, but my skin is hot and flushed.

"I always tell the truth," he says.

"You are a lewd, immodest, improper man." I'm shaking and it's not from rage, though I want to be angry.

"You were masked. No one in that room knew you." He leans forward. "Whatever you say, whatever you do with me, no one else will know that either."

His hazel eyes meet mine. The drumbeat of lust pulsing in my cunt grows to a stronger, throbbing demand. I cover my face. I can't do this. But as if with a will of their own, my legs spread beneath my skirts.

Theo pulls the curtains on both sides. Oh no. Then he transfers himself to my seat. He's so close now in the dark carriage, I can barely look at him.

His lips brush my cheek. A gentleman's kiss but he is no gentleman. He's a devil and will use a devil's tricks. I look away.

And then he's suddenly on top of me, all six feet of him, heavy with that masculine weight that feels so deliciously imprisoning. His fingers curl around my wrists and pin them back against the carriage seat, and he kisses me, his mouth warm in the cold hansom. Against all of my training, I kiss him back, feeling something in me loosen and melt.

"The driver isn't going to stop until I signal," he says, reaching behind me to unhook my dress. "We have all the time in the world."

He pushes the bodice of my dress down. I close my eyes to pretend I'm not shivering in my corset here in a public hansom. But he leans against me again, so warm and beautifully hard, and kisses me a second time, his mouth so sweet that I scarcely feel him loosening the corset. His hands pull down my chemise, fill with my breasts. And then his dark head lowers and he's sucking my nipples, a new sensation that sends stars through my blood. I arch my back against the seat.

One firm hand slides under my dress, under the petticoats. I stare in delirious awe as Theo sinks to his knees on the carriage floor and pulls down my drawers, opening my thighs wide.

His hot mouth is on my cunt a moment later, greedy and demanding, licking me so skillfully that I don't know if it's his tongue or his fingers turning my swollen flesh into melting bliss. An incoherent whimper escapes me. His talented fingers push inside me, moving in circles until they press in just the right spot. I sit up straight as sheer euphoric electricity jolts me. It sweeps through me again and again in fiery waves of glory.

He sits back on his heels, his hair rumpled. "Turn over."

"What?" I'm still dazed.

He positions me, my hands and one knee on the seat, the other foot balanced on the hansom floor. Then he throws my dress and petticoats up over my waist, and pushes his cock inside me in one slow, relentless thrust. I feel ready to split open from the massive shaft inside me. He withdraws, plunges in again. I am so wet that vulgar noises fill the carriage. But he's breathing fast, and he begins to fuck me in a savage rhythm, driving in and out until we're both panting and wet, the carriage windows steamed. My long black hair has tumbled out of its twist and my nipples are still exposed and hard as he drives me forward with every thrust. He grips my hips with a growl, spearing in and out of me so hard that I feel as if my entire body is a burning, hungry ember.

"Please," I say because I don't know how to say anything else. I'm gasping and clutching at the cushion.

"Please what." He's going to come soon, I can tell by his thick voice.

"I want to—I want to see you..." Despite being naked and fucked and utterly at his mercy, I can't say it. But Theo understands. He withdraws and flips me onto my back, dress still around my waist, and rams me again and again while I gaze up at him in his disheveled, panting glory. And then it's happening again. My skin fills with glorious white-hot light, and I scream as I begin coming in violent waves with his cock still fucking me.

Only as those waves lessen does he let go with a long groan and reach his end inside me. He falls on top of me immediately after.

"There's no hurry," he murmurs, snuggling into me. Both of us are damp and hot. "Let him keep driving."

Soon I'll adjust my corset, secure my hair. I'll bid Theo goodnight as if he's any gentleman escorting me home from the ballet, and I'll go into my quiet home and up to bed. He will—if not tomorrow, soon—move on from New York with Madame Morgana and their séance theatre. But I won't return to life as usual. A new century is dawning, and I'm going to rise like the sun.

# OPHELIA THE SECOND

by Jade A. Waters

Hamlet had the most beautiful eyes I'd ever seen.

It was almost as if our casting director had chosen him for those eyes alone. Brooding, dark and mesmerizing, they were half the magic of his performance. Night after night he stunned full houses with that penetrating gaze, capturing the essence of his character until his terrible, tragic end.

His performance itself was magical, too, but I was so far past this after years of watching Philip act. Instead, I was lost in his tormented expression as he lamented and soliloquized to the darkened house, the tiniest beads of sweat forming along his temples under the burning stage lights. He practiced with me backstage, but often I hovered in the wings, silently admiring his movements. I'd memorized his lines, and I mouthed them as he spoke them. I knew everything he did by heart, really—the way he extended his right arm here, held his left fist aloft for emphasis there and stomped his foot to draw a gasp from the audience in the middle of his first monologue. It was like he'd lived his whole life to play this role. Despite the stark contrast in their personalities, Philip was Hamlet, and it was those eyes of his that linked them, not as windows to his soul, but to the character he'd captured straight from the tattered pages of his script.

But this is how I felt about Ophelia and me—she was sweet and tender, a lost girl who died without love at every performance. Each night as I caressed the curtains, watching Philip's glorious movements across the stage, I knew this in my heart.

Ophelia, deep down, was me.

Still, the reality was that Ophelia never got to have her love. She yearned, she obsessed, she went mad.

And then she fell out of a damn tree and died.

This is what preoccupied me as Philip opened the passenger-side door for me. He ran his fingers through his rich, wavy hair, and then reached out for my hand.

"Well? You coming?"

I tried to calm the thump in my chest, just like I always did when we got together outside of Esquire. I'd had a crush on him since I joined the community theater, but he'd been dating Tammy. Ever since, everything there seemed to be about Tammy. Tammy the star. Tammy the diva.

Tammy, otherwise known as Ophelia.

Tonight we'd ended up at Philip's apartment. Somehow, I—Ophelia the Second—was walking up to his front door, watching his ass as he led me up the stairs. He'd changed plans en route to the bar, suggesting we go back to his place to drink bourbon and run lines—as if he needed practice. As if I would ever play the role of someone I longed to be.

Tammy had been playing Ophelia for four months, and she reminded me every night that this was her role and I would never need to worry about taking over. I was merely the understudy: Ophelia the Second, Ophelia the Lesser. It was Tammy's name that was printed on every program and across all the theater boards. She was Tammy Danes, community darling, headlining act and the lead actress in each play the Esquire Theatre had produced in the last five years.

She was also Philip's ex-girlfriend.

Oh, we'd seen their drama everywhere—in the green room, in the parking lot, even on stage in rehearsals. It had been two years since their breakup, and while Philip kept himself tempered and humbled without needing Robert, our director, to remind them to knock it off, Tammy regularly made a scene. I knew the grief she caused him because he vented to me, his eyes bleeding the same tortured pain as Hamlet's while he told me he wanted to escape her endless barbs and bitter commentary, and be with someone who loved like he did.

Philip opened the door to his house, pausing beneath the porch light to grin at me. When I smiled back, he brushed his hand along my cheek.

"Have I ever told you that you have the cutest smile, kid?"

Philip guided me inside before I could speak. I don't know what I would have said if I hadn't felt the sudden glue of my tongue to the roof of my mouth, either. There was no point in getting carried away with my thoughts of Philip. I'd hoped that becoming better friends with him would get me over my crush, but instead I felt like the theater girl of my early college years, swooning over another cast member in unrequited love.

It was ridiculous, really. Just as ridiculous as hoping Tammy would get laryngitis and I might finally have a night to be the real Ophelia.

Philip shut the door behind us and headed into his kitchen. His house was exactly what I'd expected, modern and tidy, with acting awards lining one of the shelves of a bookcase filled with scripts and plays. His husky rubbed against my leg as Philip poured my drink, and when I sat down on the couch, the pup curled beside my feet. I patted his head until Philip took a seat next to me, extending my glass with a wink.

"We always end up on a couch together, have you noticed?"

I laughed, trying to ignore the delicious smell of his post-show sweat, and the way the couch dipped under his sturdy, muscular body, almost pulling me into his side. He'd changed after curtain into jeans and a button-up shirt with the fanciest of shoes, and he looked even more impressive in his modern garb than he did in his lace-up leather doublet and boots.

"Guess so," I said.

I sipped the bourbon. It was hot going down, warming me more than I already was sitting in Philip's apartment with him staring at me with those heavy Hamlet eyes. I attempted to ignore the fight of my heart. I was usually strong enough to resist these terribly silly impulses around him, but it was impossible not to want him, not to imagine Hamlet speaking to me, or Philip taking my hand, pining for my love like his character did later on for Ophelia.

I suddenly felt like her—a naïve girl caught in the throes of some wild vision. It wasn't madness, though it felt like it as he surveyed me.

"Good show tonight, huh?" I asked, needing yet again to get out of my head.

"Yeah. Tammy was on fire."

I propped my elbow on the back of the couch and frowned. He knew I didn't want to hear about Tammy or her wonderful efforts playing Ophelia—I'd confessed it over brews a month ago when he took me out to celebrate a five-star review from one of the most critical journalists in the business. For some reason, Philip had been more surprised at the review than my frustrated comments with Tammy's rude backstage behavior.

"But it makes sense—whenever she's a maniac off stage, she's prepped for the role."

I snickered, a loose spiral of my hair falling in my face. Philip caught it in his fingers and brushed it back, and I stared at him, surprised.

"We should have been on stage together," he murmured.

I shrugged.

"Robert's going to come around, Nat. Hopefully with the next show. You've got the talent."

"You're sweet," I said. I took another swallow of my drink and placed the glass on his coffee table. Philip caught my hand.

"I saw you in the wings tonight."

I froze. I'd been subtle, and he'd been so into his role I couldn't imagine how he'd seen me.

"You know I see you there, right? Mouthing the lines, both mine and Ophelia's."

He clasped my hand in his and a fire sparked deep in my belly. Had the bourbon gone to his head?

Had it gone to mine?

"I'm convinced my best moments on stage are with you watching."

"That's silly," I said, but Philip nodded enthusiastically.

"You should have been Ophelia. You're perfect for the part. Your hair, your face. Everything about you, Nat—so charming and lovely."

I trembled in his grasp. Like Ophelia, I had to be going mad. Philip brushed back my curls, lifting the hair on the nape of my neck.

"Let's run lines for you."

"Why? Tammy is Ophelia, and she's never going to miss a performance. Remember?"

"Tammy is a terrible Ophelia. And one night, she will." He tapped my nose. "Come on. Let's practice."

"I need a script."

"No you don't," he said. He shoved back the table and crawled to his knees, ushering his husky off to his bed along the wall.

And then he started running lines, beginning with Act III, Scene 1, right when Ophelia meets Hamlet. He said his first line seriously, as if we were actually on stage, and I shook my head at him.

"You're crazy."

Philip frowned. "I'm trying to prove a point. You're an actress, let's go. Play along."

I'd been on the stage many times. I'd graduated with a theater degree, after all, but my parts at Esquire had been minimal, with Tammy being the star she was. Sometimes, her rants backstage and constant insults made it easy to forget that I was once a big part of productions, too.

"Well?" Philip nudged my leg and took my hand again, and I tried to ignore the peal of my heart.

"Fine," I said.

We ran through this scene, Philip's hand clasped around my shaking fingers the entire time. He was theatrical and gorgeous, his brow furrowing and his nostrils flaring at all the appropriate moments. When he peered into my face, I witnessed the same brooding depth he cast over the audience each night, except this time, it was directed at me.

This time, he was Hamlet—and I was Ophelia.

It was easy to fall into the part. I knew the lines, and he was brilliant, drawing emotion and depth into my voice that I never could when I practiced on my own in my apartment. Not without someone acting against me, getting as into the role as he did. He was magnificent. When we finished the scene, he stroked his fingertips across my palm with an encouraging nod. Then his lips turned up to form the incredibly charming grin the audience never got to see.

"Lady, shall I lie in your lap?"

I giggled. "Okay, I get it. Great scene. We can stop, though, I know the lines."

"See," he said. "You *are* the perfect Ophelia."

I rolled my eyes and Philip leaned closer, the movement catching my breath in my throat. Both of us were quiet as he crouched on the carpet. For some reason, the way he'd touched my cheek at his front door crossed my mind. Then the way he'd grinned at me at intermission, and all the times we'd hung out backstage when he'd told me he loved talking to me. My pulse raced a little quicker.

Had I missed something in my Ophelia obsession?

Philip curved his hands around my knees, increasing the pace of my heartbeat.

"And what a fair thought to lie between this maid's legs."

"That's not the line," I whispered. The look on his face was different—not Hamlet. Not Philip. It was sweet and smitten, like the one I'd seen him wear as Romeo last year. I swallowed the lump in my throat as he inched his mouth closer to mine.

"You're right. It's not."

I'd never seen him more handsome.

"You're perfect, Nat."

This had to be a dream—an Ophelia-inspired daydream that I had somehow wandered into.

But then Philip kissed me.

His lips, like his hands, were soft on my skin, and I surrendered to the press of his mouth. When I parted my lips, the tip of his tongue grazed mine and sent tingles down my spine. I opened wider, letting him in, and then we were kissing with all the passion I imagined Ophelia would have shared with Hamlet if she'd had the chance.

"God, I've wanted to kiss you for months," he whispered between kisses.

I couldn't move, couldn't breathe. Philip climbed onto the couch, taking me into his arms.

"But more, I've wanted to be alone with you. Really alone with you, Nat—no drama, no Esquire chaos..."

His kiss was fast to my lips as he guided me back against the armrest. I trembled as his hands roamed my sides, then my breasts, caressing me like I'd dreamed of more than I'd ever dreamed of being Ophelia. When Philip caught the hem of my shirt, I flashed him an eager smile.

He drew it over my head and traced his fingers across my belly, then my bra, his dark, Hamlet eyes poring over me. My pussy flooded with heat, and I shivered with the depth of his gaze. He looked as serious as he did on stage, except happier and more lustful. I grabbed at his shirt and unbuttoned it down to his waist, the sweetest whiff of him filling my nose as I exposed more of his skin. When Philip shrugged the fabric off his shoulders, he stunned me with the chest I'd seen so many times backstage—but this time naked with me. He lay over my body, slipping his hands beneath my torso and unclasping my bra, then sucked my nipple into his mouth until I moaned.

"You're lovely," he said, palming my other breast. "A beautiful, modern Ophelia."

I closed my eyes, escorted into his vision of me while he kissed my skin, then unfastened my jeans. My heart drummed as he tugged at them, urging me to lift my hips so he could pull them off and to the floor. When he dipped his face between my thighs I gasped at the hot air he blew through the lace of my panties. Philip breathed against me for an eternity, enticing me with slow teases of his tongue as I pawed at his head. Finally, he grabbed the waistband of my panties and looked up at me.

"May I lie between your legs, Nat?"

I whimpered in encouragement, my blood swishing in my ears as Philip eased the panties down my thighs, then off over my feet. His tongue was quick to my sex, circling my clit and lapping at my slick folds as he glided his hands over my belly and across my breasts. I bucked up against him, the effort of his mouth driving me to the precipice of ecstasy and drawing wild sighs from my throat.

The awareness that my crush on him was real and mutual, coming to life like he did on stage, rushed into me almost as swiftly as my lust for him. I clutched at his hair and neck, delighting in his ferocity and aching to feel him inside, to consummate this play between us. "Philip, please," I cried.

Philip groaned, then stood. He peeled down the last of his clothes, and I pressed my fingertips over my mouth. I'd seen him in his briefs on occasion backstage, but it was nothing like this—his body shadowed with the dim glow of his kitchen light and his cock swollen and thick, exposed to me. He stepped out of the pile of clothes at his feet, his body gorgeous and firm as he crouched at my hip.

"Are you sure?"

I gripped his thigh with a whisper.

"Oh yes."

Swiftly, Philip fished his wallet from his slacks and withdrew a condom. He sheathed himself and crawled onto the couch, his knee rubbing against my cunt, making me roll my hips in desperation. I curved my fingertips around his shoulders to steer him closer, and Philip guided the head of his cock to my wetness.

"Be my Ophelia," he said.

"Yes." I curled my arms around him, lost in this role we were playing. I was Ophelia to his Hamlet, Nat to his Philip. He pushed forward, anchoring the tip of his length inside me and sending spasms through my walls. "God, yes, yes, yes."

Philip thrust hard then, sinking all the way into me with a groan. His lips fell to mine as he groped at my sides, then swooped his hands beneath me to clutch my back. His strokes were long and deep, filling me as if he'd craved me, needed me. Like it wasn't me aching to be with him on stage, but him aching for me to be there, acting alongside him in the love affair that had never had a chance to be.

"You feel amazing," he said. He slid his hand between our hips, massaging my clit with the pads of his fingers as he kissed me. The heat spilled from my folds and throughout my body, a surge of passion that rocked my core.

"Philip!" I moaned. He thrust into me, again and again, his lips heavy on mine until I cried out in ecstasy, clawing at his back as he rode the convulsions within me. His broad chest smothered me as he sank all the way in, and then he was grunting and panting, crying my name.

"Nat...Ophelia...God damn, *yes.*"

Crying Ophelia's name.

We lay there for several minutes, silent and gasping. My lips were tight against his chest, and he'd buried his mouth in my hair. When his length slowly retreated from inside me, Philip leaned back.

"I always wondered what would have happened if Hamlet got his Ophelia," he said.

I giggled, the contractions of my inner muscles forcing him out. Philip didn't shift away, peering down at me with his beautiful eyes.

"Me too."

He lifted his hand to my face, tenderly running his fingertip along my cheek and curling a strand of my hair around his finger. "I think, if she'd lived, he would never have let her go."

He kissed me as we lay there, and I wrapped my arms around his waist, delighting in his touch.

For now, the role of Ophelia the Second would do just fine.

# REVISITING YOUTH

by J. Crichton and H. Keyes

Aya went out that night looking to feel. She had a glass of wine
before she even started out, then put on her slinkiest black dress
and headed into the glittering lights with all of her covered up in
an unassuming trench coat. The streets of Tokyo were no place
for a woman on the prowl; she'd learned after years of practice
that going directly after what you wanted just wasn't done.

For three years her marriage had been sexless and still she'd
held out. At first she'd asked her husband every day, then every
week, then from time to time... More often than not he'd come
home late (too late) from the office, exhausted beyond belief
after working from ten in the morning to 1:00 a.m. That was
fine; he was too tired. She had to be accepting of that. Then
he'd sleep all hours of the weekend, had no time for hobbies
and begrudged her on a Sunday afternoon when she approached
him for a little afternoon delight, because it was the only time he
had to himself. Why didn't he tell his boss to screw himself and
come home so he could screw his wife, she'd asked. *You know I
can't do that*, he'd said. *It's just not done.* She'd cried and tried

to be stoic by turns, screamed at him some days and considered starring in one of those "married women gone wild!" pornos on others. Anything just to feel something again. God, how many years of silicone-based cock had she faced?

In the end she'd had to divorce him and that was less than a month ago. It still hurt, of course. She loved him and they remained friends, but friends didn't need to fuck each other and she was adamant that that was something she deserved. Forty-something and with an insatiable, unapologetic craving for affection? She was going to seek out her own satisfaction now that she had earned her freedom.

So now she was surrounded by men who could just as easily be her husband's colleagues—ex-husband's, sorry—offering to buy her tits a drink. "Can I buy you a drink?" was most often accompanied by "I'm a banker" or "I'm just here on business." The latter was code for "I've got a wife at home but we can make some sort of arrangement." It stung in the way that a half-healed wound is still tender when poked hard enough. She'd done it to herself.

She left the first bar and walked the twenty minutes it took to get to Roppongi instead. From the business district to the party district, she walked past eighties bars and booming dance clubs, people already bent in half by the roadside as they emptied their guts and friends rubbed their backs. A few hugely muscular guys offered to take her to their bars, and some others in shiny suits and wearing too much hairspray asked if she had "a little time," but she was looking for someone to love. At least for the night.

It took until she came across a simple Japanese-style pub, an *izakaya*, for her to take a seat. She was overdressed for a casual hangout that served pints of beer for a single coin, but it was different enough to spark her interest.

Seated at a four-person table alone, she placed her coat on one of the stools and discreetly adjusted her bra for maximum lift. She told the staff, who couldn't have been more than twenty years old, that she was waiting for someone. It wasn't a lie. The place was bathed in a happy, yellow light, with smoke from cigarettes and steam from hot pots rising from the tables, people laughing raucously and bragging about some exploit that had probably never happened. Little by little, she found herself smiling.

By and by she nursed a beer, and a massive group of college students arrived. Given that it was the end of March they were probably all graduating soon. Aya was situated in a corner in the back of the pub, while they stretched out at a long table across from her. She could see a row of about six guys with their backs to her, and another six facing her from a distance. No, there was one discrepancy to their group: sitting almost directly across from her was one petite, mousy girl. The realization came as a shock, although she knew they must be part of the same club at their university. They weren't huge guys, not more muscular than average, so she guessed it might be something technical or musical. Maybe even artistic, but that didn't stop the pang of jealousy Aya felt at knowing this little girl commanded the attention of twelve men.

She sipped her beer and tried to direct her attention elsewhere, but it always came back to the group right in front of her with the college girl seated second from the end. Three of the guys, the three closest to her, were chatting, trying to entertain her. Aya wondered if all three of them had a crush on her, or if the girl had spent time alone with all three of them, and then scolded herself for such uncharitable thoughts. The point was that she could remember a time when she'd been as desirable, as easygoing with men and her sexuality as this young woman out drinking with a soccer team's worth of good-looking college boys. Years of being spurned had damaged her self confidence and she was, underneath it all, terribly afraid that she would never get that sense of self back.

It took her ten minutes of glancing over, of catching the girl's eyes and having her gaze slide away again, before she found the courage to call out.

"Hey!" About half of the group turned to face her, as well as several other curious patrons at other tables. "What are you guys celebrating?" she asked, uncrossing her legs and recrossing them in the other direction. One of the loudest of the group, a fluffy-haired boy band type, grinned and stole a glance at her legs.

"We're graduating in three days. This is our last hurrah, so to speak."

"How lovely," she purred. "I'd like to buy you all a round to express my congratulations, if that's alright with you."

Murmurs of surprise rose from the group. "What, all of us?"

She fixed the second speaker, a traditional dark-haired lad with excellent posture, with a slow grin. If she was lucky, the misgivings bouncing around in her ribcage wouldn't reach her eyes. "Of course—if that's alright with you."

Cheers arose from the table, and their boisterous gathering got even louder. The young girl looked spooked, but the three who had been paying attention to her before soon turned to chat about this unexpected turn of events. What Aya hadn't expected was the three guys who shifted away from their own table and came to sit at hers.

"Budge over, *Nee-san*," said the one who had spoken first. Elder sister, that was what they called older women like Aya. He was carrying his beer and making to steal the outer seat she'd settled herself in. The other man who'd spoken held his hands out for her coat and hung it on the wall, as gentlemanly as he could. She felt a warm wash of quiet excitement and slid her satin-covered bum onto the inner stool. Now she finally felt somehow that she still had *it*, whatever it was.

"I'm Yu," said the de facto leader of their little group, "and this is Eito." He gestured to the kid with the nice posture. "And here's Ryusei. Mind if we keep you company?"

"I suppose I could handle a bit of company," she smiled. "Are you all in the same class?"

"Same extracurricular activity. We're in the snowboarding club. Or we were, I guess."

She nodded and raised her glass. "It's all ending now, huh? Soon enough you'll be dressed in your recruit suits and listening to the speeches of company presidents, staying late and dyeing your hair regulation black. It's gonna be hard, but let me tell you." She shifted closer to all of them and gestured with her glass. "Don't let them steal your hearts. Don't become that drone that still thinks he has time to live later. You'll forget how to do it."

"We'll do our best," said Yu, taking a long chug of his beer. "I know it's going to be a battle. I know. I just don't like to think about it."

Eito mumbled words of agreement, and Ryusei's jaw tightened into a stiff smile. Yu patted Eito on the shoulder comfortingly. They spoke a few more minutes about some of their club's greatest hits, and then Ryusei shifted quietly away, back to the main table.

Aya was soon snorting inelegantly about a story where the boys of the group had all decided to run towel-clad through the snow to get into a hot spring located miles away from any man-made structure in the mountains of the north.

"And? Was it worth it?" Aya smiled, remembering a few of her own college escapades. How she loved the fearlessness that came with youth.

Eito laughed outright, more openly than he had until that point. "I entered first—you know I won, Yu, don't lie—but it was the hottest thing ever! My feet felt like they'd gotten cold burnt in the snow only to be boiled in a ridiculously hot spring! Natural? Sure, but—"

"You were howling!" Yu laughed. "We all were. It was so shallow and rocky that I thought I was going to scrape my balls and—" He stopped abruptly, clamping a hand over his mouth when he realized what he'd just said. Apparently he'd said it loud enough to attract the attention of the main table as well. Aya glanced over in time to see the young girl watching her curiously.

"No! Don't be shy." She grinned, raising an eyebrow over at her younger counterpart. They could have been sisters in Aya's younger days. "Continue with your story, it was just getting juicy."

"It only came up to our waists, so our lower halves were boiling and the upper halves were freezing cold. Like sitting around in bathwater that's draining, but you don't want to get out so you sink lower and lower," Eito said, gesturing to his hips and slipping down in his chair. Aya admired the view.

His description was how she felt about life sometimes, if she was perfectly honest. There was no excuse for it anymore: no excuse for living trapped between two worlds that didn't quite suit, hoping that sliding one way or the other would make it all more comfortable. Well, sometimes you just had to head for a third option. "Makes me want to take a bath," she said instead.

Yu's eyes widened for a moment and there was a moment of delicious recognition. "Not in the wilderness though," she clarified. "I like my creature comforts—bubbles and bath jets."

Eito shifted in his seat and Aya smiled, happy to give the impression that flirting with danger could be so, so good. "Did you ever do anything like that in university?"

"Oh, what didn't we do? I remember one Halloween we went to Shibuya and I was wearing a Little Red Riding Hood costume…"

The next hour or so passed in fits of laughter and slightly tipsy leaning on one another as they skipped over the polite small talk that often accompanies meeting new people, and went straight into bold confessions of future fears and past mistakes. "I've always wanted to sleep with an older woman,"

Yu announced out of the blue, raising his arms over his head to fake a yawn. *Real smooth, kid,* thought Aya.

"Me too," Eito jumped in, a little more nervously. Aya glanced over at the main table, wondering if any of their companions had overheard. They hadn't. "Young girls are just so..." He gestured helplessly to the air.

They were pushing the envelope here; they all were, except that Aya knew a thing or two about putting your money where your mouth was. "Wanna get out of here, boys?" A thrill of excitement raced up and down her arms, down her legs, tingled in all the right places. Both of her college grads stared, open mouthed, before Yu reached for his coat. Eito leapt out of his chair, and in the space of a minute they were headed for the street. Aya didn't bother to look for the expression on the college girl's face; she left it behind, along with her inhibitions.

Half a block up the street was a love hotel, square with a couple of lit-up boards advertising by-the-hour prices and a cheesy name, but otherwise exactly like any of the apartment buildings that filled the spaces above and around the bars. The three of them hesitated in front of the automatic sliding doors that read "Front," wondering if their courage would carry them that far.

"Okay?" asked Eito, slightly breathless with exhilaration at his own bravado.

"Let's do it," Aya said confidently, leading the way. Inside there was a menu screen displaying the interiors of rooms and their prices. There were no staff visible, and the area was dimly lit enough that no one could identify them unless they were up close.

"What about that one?" said Yu, pointing to a four-poster bed in red and cream. "The bed looks wide." He giggled nervously, and Aya pressed the button before anyone let their shyness get the better of them.

Once in the room, the trio found themselves shyly winding

J. CRICHTON AND H. KEYES

their way around one another. Yu on the left and Eito to the right, Aya turned her head back and forth as the younger men kissed down her neck and over her breasts. Eito, for all his nerves, took the plunge and began running his hands over Aya's silky dress, smoothing it against the contours of her body and pressing himself to her. Aya's back arched as Yu took things a step further and slowly traced his hand over her thigh and under her dress, just skimming over the lace of her panties. The two men were practically competing with one another as Eito's hand joined in, caressing her ass, squeezing it, a soft moan telling her that she was as desirable as she'd hoped. It felt so good to be wanted like this.

Feeling the heady rush of pleasure, she pulled her dress over her head, showing her best set of lingerie to them, a set that her own ex-husband hadn't even cared to see. Moans of appreciation were followed by hurried undressing by both men; piles of clothes joined hers on the floor. Aya was impressed at the sight of the naked young men; it had been a long time since she'd seen a hard body in person, much less two of them—and they were both wonderfully hard in other ways as well.

Naked, the trio laid on the crisp white sheets of the queen-size bed and explored one another slowly, tantalizingly. There were hands everywhere, mouths too, and the sensations were almost too much. Aya sat up and turned to look at the two men, Eito with his thick, ever-so-slightly curved cock standing straight up, and Yu, a bare fraction of an inch smaller but lying flat against his belly, the head sticky with precome.

Aya grinned and gestured for the two men to move closer together as she brushed her hair back and knelt between them. She wrapped her hands around both of their cocks, enjoying the texture of hard but velvety flesh, and very slowly, deliberately stroked them up and down, her eyes flitting back and forth between the two, judging their reactions. Eito was watching her intently, his stomach muscles tightening with each movement of her hands, while Yu's eyes were closed, his head flat against the pillow and his mouth open in a pant. Without breaking her rhythm, Aya locked eyes with Eito and took his cock in her mouth, her tongue flattening as she slid the shaft into her throat, the salty juices mixing with her saliva as she swallowed hungrily. Eito gave an involuntary thrust, his balls pushing against her chin as she rolled her tongue over the head. All the while, her palm stroked over Yu's; he was very sensitive, she realized, and it wouldn't take much for him to come all over if she wasn't careful. Slowly she lifted her head and released Eito with a slurp and switched to Yu, her tongue darting back and forth over the base of his cock, avoiding the head as much as she could.

Aya could have kept going for hours, the taste of the two men mixing in her mouth, but Yu had other plans. While she was back to deep-throating Eito, Yu gently disengaged her hand and slid down the bed, his hands nudging her thighs apart before he crawled under her. Yu pulled her hips down, taking some of the weight off her knees as he buried his mouth and tongue in her dripping wet pussy. Aya moaned around Eito's cock as Yu's lips brushed over her clit; he was kissing it, then lapping at her lips, then shaking his head.

Where had a man of his age learned such things, she wondered, as Eito's hands pulled her head down farther onto his twitching length. Yu had found her most sensitive spot and she shuddered; the cock in her mouth and the sensations between her legs were overpowering. Now that Yu had found her weakness, he was holding her down, his fingers gripping her hips, and Aya was done for. She came forcefully, ripples of electricity skipping down her back and through her pussy, the lips shuddering against Yu's onslaught. Eito sat up, freeing Aya's mouth while his hands strayed to her nipples, rolling them mercilessly as she shook; this only served to intensify her orgasm and she sank into it, letting her voice echo around the room.

Unable to feel her legs, much less move, Aya allowed the men to help her onto her side between the them, Yu behind and Eito in front. They looked at one another over her shoulder, seemingly to check whether they were both satisfied with their positions, when Eito reached down and lifted Aya's leg up into the air, holding her wide open. Yu's chest pressed into her back then his cock slid inside her; he pushed lazily, coating himself in her juices while his hand held her steady. Eito watched in silence as Yu fucked her, then took himself in hand and began stroking the head of his penis against her already aching clit. His precome added to the mixture, Aya was saturated and after the briefest of teases, Eito lifted her leg higher and pushed himself in, the two men sharing her slit. The bizarre combination of two cocks rubbing against one another inside her, thrusting in different rhythms against every inch of her was overwhelming.

She was stretched to the limit; it was almost painful, but so, so pleasurable at the same time. Yu was jackhammering against her, his mouth leaving sticky kisses over her shoulder and down the back of her neck, while Eito was barely moving, just pushing himself from deep to deeper inside. They were focused on their own pleasure, so much so that neither seemed to notice when Aya's hand went to her clit, needing only the barest of touches to start herself clenching, albeit a much more challenging feat around two willful men. Both seemed to change pace then, Yu slowing down as Eito sped up; they were very nearly in sync when Aya cried out in her third orgasm of the evening. Eito buried himself within her and growled as he came; she could feel the thick ropes of come hitting the front wall of her pussy, and the way his balls twitched against her as he emptied himself. Yu, on the other hand, sank his teeth into her shoulder as he thrust through his release, each splash punctuated by the slap of his stomach against her ass.

Satiated, sleepy, the three lovers lay there lost in their individual moments until their bodies cooled and Aya could feel the telltale slick oozing out of her thoroughly yet happily abused pussy. Eito's arm had slunk around her, and his hand was lazily squeezing her breast when Yu sat up, scrubbed his face with his hands and then disappeared momentarily, before returning with a fluffy white towel just barely hanging off his hips. "You said you wanted a bath," he grinned, "so let's go."

Adventures, Aya realized, only stop happening when you stop looking for them.

# DATE NIGHT

## by D.R. Slaten

"Is this seat taken?" a low male voice asked.

"No," she replied without looking up.

She felt him take a seat. She didn't even look at him. She just looked at her drink, lost in her thoughts.

"Are you here alone?"

"Yes," she replied. This time she looked up.

She was met with gorgeous green eyes. A dark, mossy green color, flecked with brown. She watched his pupils dilate. His eyes weren't the only gorgeous thing about him. Strong jaw. Strong male features generally. But the mouth—the mouth was lush. Full. Pink. Not dark pink, a lighter version, strawberry-lemonade pink. Those lips totally contrasted with the rest of him.

"Are..." She had to clear her throat. Saliva had pooled as she'd inspected him, catching in the back of her throat and making it impossible to continue to talk. "Are you here alone?"

"Yes," he told her.

He didn't avert his gaze. He stared straight at her. Even

though his eyes didn't move, she had the feeling that he saw all of her anyway, that he was taking her in, drinking her down. He didn't need to glance at her breasts or her ass to indicate he was attracted. He just was. And she knew it.

Maybe it was the way his pupils kept dilating and his eyes kept opening. Or the slight flaring of his nostrils as he took in her scent. Unspoken, his body was communicating with hers in a multitude of minute ways. She knew hers was as well.

"Oh." She couldn't think of anything else to say. Her brain had short-circuited.

The bartender walked over, silently waiting for his drink order.

"Oban. No ice. No water," he ordered.

"You have good taste in scotch," she said. Another inane comment. Shit, she was going to sound like she was a half-wit if this kept up.

"I like to think so." His mouth tipped up slightly.

He picked up the glass the bartender had delivered and brought it to his mouth. Taking a small sip, she watched as he swallowed. His Adam's apple bobbed in one smooth motion, not jerky like she saw on some men.

Getting turned on by a man's Adam's apple had never happened to her before. She was at a loss for words at this newfound interest. It bordered on kinky. It bordered on the absurd. Maybe it was a cross: kinkily absurd. Or absurdly kinky. She wasn't sure. Whatever it was, it was just wrong to have such a thing shoot a tingle through her body.

"Do you come here often?" he asked, looking around the bar.

It was a lounge really. A place for businesspeople to drop in after work, before the night crowd showed up for the meat market. A small cottage set in the middle of a large urban area. It even featured a bocce ball lawn next to the outdoor seating area.

"No. I was at loose ends. Got tired of being stuck at home. Decided to get out and my feet brought me here," she answered. "You?"

"Me either," he said. "Although now, I'm wondering why." Zing. Total pickup line. He was flirting with her. Holy-hot guy was flirting with her.

She took a drink of her cosmo, stalling for time before she needed to respond. The last thing she wanted to do was say something stupid again. Apparently, her witty, sparkling self had taken a hiatus when she saw holy-hot guy, leaving her bumbling and tongue-tied. Maybe he would notice her tits instead of her less-than-erudite self. That would be good.

She finished her cosmo and signaled for another.

"Where do you normally go if not here?" she asked. Whew, at least that didn't sound stupid. It sounded like she was interested in learning more about him. No, not stupid at all.

"I'm a homebody," he said. "I putter around my house. Bars and stuff aren't really my scene."

"I totally get that," she replied, keeping her answer short and hopefully less socially awkward.

The booze was hitting her. Vodka always went straight to her head. Then it traveled through her body, leaving a nice, warm glow in its wake. She'd have to nurse her next cosmo because if she drank more than two, she would not make good decisions at all.

As they chatted, he finished off his drink as well. For one minute she feared he would pay his tab and leave now that the scotch was gone, but he didn't. When he signaled for another, she let out a huge internal sigh of relief. Thank Christ he wasn't leaving, because that would completely suck. She was diggin' on him. And she thought he was diggin' on her.

"Are you seeing someone? Hooked with anyone? Um, sleeping with someone? Shit, I don't even know the correct terminology anymore, I've been out of the dating scene so long," she said as her brain totally panicked at his earlier comment about being a homebody. There was only one reason someone as hot as he was stayed at home, and it wasn't because the ball game was on.

His laugh was low; it reverberated through her body, figuratively and literally. He'd shifted slightly closer to her, enough so she could feel the heat he was putting off and the rumble of his laugh.

"Not tonight," he said.

Dare she ask? Did she care? Umm, yeah. Not so much. So she left it alone. She knew what she wanted. A wrong answer to any question she posed and she'd be ethically bound by girl-club rules about staying away from taken men. But he'd said he wasn't taken tonight. Good enough. There had to be a super-secret exemption to the girl-club rules when it was holy-hot guy and he wasn't involved for the evening. There were lots of potential reasons for that, but none she wanted to examine too closely.

"I need to go to the restroom," she said. Then she decided to be bold and daring. "Um, you wanna go somewhere more private to talk?"

Shit, she'd done it again. "Talk" was a euphemism for a lot of things. God, she was a huge dork. Her dating muscles were definitely out of practice. Completely flaccid.

He gave her a long look. This time he didn't stop his eyes from traveling over her body. He had an unobstructed view since she'd stood up before announcing her intention to slip away to the bathroom.

Her dress was killer and enhanced her body in every way. The short cut emphasized what was probably her best feature—her legs—though the long-sleeve, turtleneck style covered most of her body. A pair of plain black stilettos completed the look, further showcasing her legs. Even without a "perfect" body, she knew how to play up her gams.

She could tell he liked her legs. His eyes flared when they surveyed her lower half. Something about long legs on a woman made men hot. It was a good thing, at least for her. If he was picturing her legs doing all manner of naughty things, then he might say yes to going somewhere and "talking."

"Yeah, I want that," he said. His eyes remained glued to her legs.

She drained the last of her cosmo. By then, his eyes had come back up to look at her face, but only for a moment because she turned to walk to the bathrooms in the back of the lounge.

Bernie's was a quirky bar. One door to the bathroom read "heartfull" while the other read "heartless." No simple "boys" and "girls." She picked heartless. It was huge. Much bigger than any single bathroom she'd ever seen at a bar.

She couldn't believe she'd been so forward. It wasn't like her. She blamed the damn drinks; obviously vodka and cranberry juice had given her more than a buzz. It had given her courage—and a full bladder. One of those things she'd already taken care of. The other, she was about to take care of.

After peeing, she washed her hands and went to open the door. Holy-hot guy was on the other side. She was at a loss for words. She hadn't expected him there.

He didn't wait for her invitation. He entered the bathroom, locking it behind him.

"I paid the tab. Let's talk," he said.

She had nothing to say. Every thought she'd ever had fled in the wake of the predicament of being alone with him behind a closed and locked door. They looked at each other, evaluating the situation—but not for long.

He pulled her to him. She went. He had his mouth on hers in the blink of an eye. Smoky, smooth scotch overlaid the very distinctive taste of man. Of him. She moaned. He tasted fantastic. His tongue tingled her lips as it brushed past to delve into her mouth. Locked in the give and take of sharing a breath, his tongue swept past her teeth to touch and be touched by her tongue, a delicate dance of in and out. Forward and retreat. Tasting. Teasing. Tormenting.

In contrast to the frantic meeting of their mouths, he gently braced her back against the wall, making sure she didn't slam up against it.

This was yin and yang, his hard body pushing into her softening one. She could feel her pussy preparing for him. The telltale wetness between her legs increased by the minute. He pushed her thighs apart with his leg, pressing against her mound, the pressure exquisite yet not enough.

When he felt her heat, her dampness, he groaned. "You are so fucking hot. I can't stop thinking about your goddamn legs. They must go on forever."

She couldn't speak. That skill had left her. Her eyes had drifted to half mast as she delighted in the pressure of being sandwiched between him and the wall.

As her thighs spread, her dress rode up. His hand moved to the juncture between her legs. He stepped his other leg in between hers, widening her stance, as his hand caressed her thin silk panties.

"Are you wet?" he asked, knowing full well she was. The evidence was under his hand.

"Yes," she said through her swollen mouth, glistening still from their kiss.

"Christ, your pussy feels like an inferno. It's gonna burn my hand." His breathing was becoming more uneven.

He moved his hand into her underwear, his fingers moving over her clit. She jerked at the contact. A small whimper escaped her mouth. A huge conflagration ignited at his touch, bursting through her body.

At that moment, she didn't care that she was in a lounge bathroom, several people on the other side of the door. The entire focus of her existence centered on his hand: the warmth of it as it rested against her skin, the texture of his fingers as they moved against her clit. Even if she'd wanted to pull back, his legs made it impossible to close herself from him. She was open, wide. He ruthlessly exploited her predicament.

Her head moved back against the wall, exposing her neck. His mouth was on it in a second later, kissing and licking her, tasting and feeling her. She knew the beat of the pulse in her neck had quickened. The blood had rushed to her pussy so fast—maybe that's why she was lightheaded, she thought.

He couldn't kiss too far down her throat—the turtleneck got in his way—so he suckled the exposed flesh, contenting himself with that part of her for now.

As his fingers moved from rubbing her clit like it was a magical genie lamp, she moaned in protest, but sighed as soon as two fingers moved into her passage, massaging her intimately. He angled the palm of his hand to over her clit, giving her needed friction to take her to paradise. He scissored his fingers on the withdrawal and closed them back up as he moved them into her.

Finally, he pushed them until they came to the depth behind her pubic bone. Curling them up slightly against her spongy flesh, he applied pressure to her clit with his palm at the same time. She felt the first radiation of electrical pulse-like jolts move in an outward radius from between her legs. Her hands moved up to massage her breasts over her clothes, helping those jolts turn into tingles.

He pulled back.

"No," she protested. "I'm close. No. Please. Don't stop."

"Tell me you want me. Tell me I can have you. Tell me yes," he whispered against her ear as he brought his mouth up from the middle of her throat. He pulled back so he could see her face. It was flushed with desire, her mouth dry from need. She licked her parched lips.

"Yes, please yes. Please," she breathed out. "Please."

She heard her underwear ripping. She hadn't felt anything.

Didn't know his hands had moved to remove the barrier between them. Next she heard the rasp of his zipper.

As his cock slid between the lips of her pussy, he moved his hand around to her ass. He lifted her up slightly until he could fully lodge the head of his cock at her entrance. She was so wet, nothing prevented him from sliding fully into her as she slid down and he powered up.

"Fuck, you feel so good," he told her.

"It's the same for me. Please. Too good. I need you to move. I'm too close," she begged.

He moved then. With purpose and with force, fucking into her in long, deep thrusts. Almost all the way out, before he snapped his hips to push back in. His mouth sucked her earlobe in, worrying it as he moved in her.

"Oh god. You feel so good."

She opened her eyes slightly, and then all the way. She was shocked as she saw their reflection in the mirror across the room. They looked wanton. The picture they made spiked her arousal. She didn't know how that could be—she was already at the peak of anything she'd ever felt. She watched as his ass flexed when he pushed back into her.

She was holding onto his shoulders with both hands as he lodged his cock into her. Still watching him fuck her, she gripped him harder. She needed this to end.

Her skin felt too tight. Her body felt too tight. She was almost to the point of overload and she needed to come, more than she needed her next breath. If she'd been given a choice at that moment to breathe or come, she would have chosen to suffocate. Hands down.

Her fingers reached her clit. It didn't take much at that point. She crested, crashing to the other side as everything inside her exploded in a moment of blinding pleasure. He moved his mouth over hers, absorbing the low, animalistic moan she released as she came into him.

His mouth plundered. Nothing else described the way he ate at her mouth. Hungry for her taste, hungry to receive the sounds of her pleasure.

Instead of throwing back his head to groan out his release, he gave his pleasure noise to her. Staying melded to her mouth, he jammed his cock inside her as hard as he could. Very soon, he was jerking and pulsing inside her.

Moments passed; they could have been a lifetime as far as she was concerned. The bathroom was an oasis of silence and labored breathing. The silence remained as they regained their breath together.

He gently released her legs. She slid them down with him still inside her. He stayed next to her as she regained her equilibrium.

"Let me get something to clean you up," he told her.

He'd come inside her. In a bathroom. In a bar.

He withdrew slowly, almost as if he were loathe to leave her body. She in turn was loathe to have him leave.

As soon as he was out, she felt the gush of their combined fluids slipping from her. He hurried to the paper towel dispenser, wet some down and brought them back to her. Then he cleaned her. Softly. Reverently.

He kissed the top of her pussy when he was done, then threw the paper towels into the trash.

She pulled her dress down and looked at herself in the mirror, righting her hair and smoothing her hands over her body.

He'd already put his cock back into his pants.

He turned to her.

"I love you," he said.

"I know. I love you too," she told him. "Thank you for doing this. Thank you for making my fantasy come true."

"Anything, Lyssa." His face was soft as he gazed at her. Then his mouth moved into a full grin. "Next week's date night is mine. So be prepared."

She giggled. "I can't wait."

He took her hand. "Let's go home, honey. I'm not done by a long shot."

"Okay," she agreed. These date nights were fun. And they kept their marriage interesting. Especially the sex—the sex rocked when they played out their fantasies. "Take me home."

# FLYING SOLO

by Rachel Kramer Bussel

I've made sure my camera has plenty of battery left for this trip, because you're not here to watch me. I wish you were, but life sometimes keeps us apart. You didn't ask me to, but I want to send you photos of me naked, turned on, wet for you. Even though you're not talking up a storm as you usually are when we travel, I feel you with me as I pass through security, and especially as I head to the gate and start casually, quietly, discreetly looking around, the way we did on our honeymoon. Has it really been four years? They've flown by.

I'll never forget sitting with you and hearing you whisper, "Find someone to take back to our hotel room with us." You didn't specify if it should be a man or a woman, and although I'd never considered it before, the idea of being pressed between you and another man made me so excited I almost spilled the medium coffee I'd just purchased. You took it from my hand and blew through the small opening in the plastic top for me, raising your eyebrows. I giggled, then started looking. I reached for your hand for support; you squeezed it but then let me go.

I fiddled with my wedding ring, twisting around the new gold band over and over, afraid I looked like a kid in a candy store.

You'd whispered to me again. "I'm just so madly in love with you, and I think this should be a new tradition; when we travel, we find someone to join us. Just for fun, no strings attached." I'd spent the entire time before we boarded perusing every adult sitting around us, mentally undressing them, wondering who had piercings or tattoos, who was kinky, who was the best kisser. I pictured the tall man in a suit, speaking rapidly in Spanish on the phone, with his cock in your mouth. I pictured the short, curvy beauty with her head buried between my legs while you entered her from behind.

"Well?" you'd asked, as they started to board the plane.

"I can't decide. And I certainly can't go up to any of these people. What am I going to say? 'I just got married and my husband wants to have a threesome?'" Yet even saying those unspeakable words made me wet, made my mind and heart race. I'd told you that I was bisexual after our third date, wanting to make sure you wouldn't have that awful, frat-boy, "That's hot!" reaction that even most seemingly sophisticated men busted out once I revealed I went both ways. You just nodded and let me tell you all about Simone, the gorgeous woman with the smoky voice and beautiful, curvy body I'd most recently bedded.

I'd fallen in love with you in part because you let me tell you anything, and in turn revealed some of your fantasies. We'd tried out many of them—bondage, strap-ons, hot wax. We'd talked about threesomes and orgies but in a fantasy way, until that trip. For whatever reason, you'd never mentioned wanting to be with another man, but I liked learning new things about you just when I thought I knew it all. "Let's wait until we're on the plane," I'd said, and lucky me: my dream girl, the one whose face I kept returning to, was sitting next to me on the plane. You'd pretended to sleep while I made small talk with her, all the while working up the courage to say what I most wanted to. As it turned out, she'd been the one to whisper in my ear, "I wish I could be alone with you for an hour. I want to kiss you all over."

I'd stared right back at her, barely hearing the screaming infant behind us, or the blaring music from the woman's headphones in front of us. I just saw her, Katia, her ripe, naturally pink lips, her jet-black hair, the tiny diamond glinting from her lightly freckled nose. When I reached up and traced her lips, you'd stirred, gently knocking my knee with yours. "You can. Well, not alone, exactly. I'm with him," I'd whispered, getting close enough to make sure my lips grazed her earlobe. "It's our honeymoon, but he wants me to bring someone home for us to share."

"I'm good at sharing," she'd whispered back, and she'd proven exactly how good once we were settled into our suite. Fresh from a hot shower we'd shared, our kisses making me tingle all over, Katia had gotten you and me on our backs and eased her mouth from one to the other until I was absolutely dripping wet, desperate for more. "You get on top of him," she'd instructed, in the sweetest, silkiest voice possible. It was an order, but a gentle one. If I'd had a better plan I'm sure she'd have gone along with it, but there was nothing I wanted more than your cock inside me, my body primed from her hot, hungry tongue. She eased you inside me and just as I moaned and thought I might come right then and there, her tongue was back, lapping between the cheeks she held open with those soft, delicate hands. Her tongue pressed against my rosebud, making me groan.

"She's licking me," I'd whispered frantically before burying my face in your neck. She worked me into a frenzy, one that your hard, driving cock only made more frantic. When Katia's fingers reached around me to circle my clit, I came, trembling against both of you, then biting your neck when her fingers didn't stop dancing against my hard bud. She raised her head, only to nip at the soft flesh of my ass while she coaxed another climax from me. But it wasn't until she lifted me off of you, pressed three fingers deep inside me, then eased them out and put them in your mouth that I really lost it. The look of sheer ecstasy on your face had me slamming down on top of you, fucking you harder than I ever had. You looked right at me while you sucked her fingers, and I came for the third time, something I'd also never done.

"Can I taste him?" she'd asked, and no sooner were the words out of her mouth than I was climbing off of you, wrapping my hand around the base of your cock, and feeding it to her. She didn't swallow the whole thing greedily like I would have. Instead, Katia was like a cat with a bowl of milk, her tongue slowly licking up the cream at the tip, one long stroke at a time. I'd never seen a woman give a blow job up close like that, and I didn't even think about what I did next, I just leaned forward and joined her, my tongue on one side of the ridged crown, hers on the other. Soon we were taking turns putting the head in our mouths, but I let her do the honors when you started to buck your hips up and down. I was too blissed out to give you the proper care and devotion you deserved, but Katia certainly wasn't. I saw her saliva glinting off the length of your shaft as she rose all the way up, opened those beautiful brown eyes to stare at me, then, keeping her gaze locked on mine, moved all the way down. When I reached out to stroke her hair, you grabbed my hand and we both put just a little pressure on her head, enough to make her moan. Soon you were fucking her face—there's no other way to describe it. She was grunting like an animal and you were lost in the feel of her mouth.

If someone had told me I'd spend the first night of my honeymoon watching another woman giving my husband head—and liking it—a few years before, or even a few weeks before, I'd have thought they were crazy. But in the moment, it was the hottest thing ever. There was no separation between us; we were all connected by our desire, our yearning to give and get pleasure all at the same time. When you came, I could tell instantly, even though Katia expertly sucked down every drop. "I think you should let Katia sit on your face," you told me. Oh my goodness. Of course. I lay back and soon she was on top of me, not writhing wildly, but slowly pressing herself against my mouth, enveloping my senses with her perfume. You got between my legs and ate me while I ate her, and even though your tongue distracted me from what I was doing, nobody minded. Eventually her languid movements weren't enough for me, and I pulled her tight against me, loving how wet she was getting, loving it even more when she came. She repeated her clit stroking as you kept your mouth on me, so I got to experience a fourth orgasm that knocked me out. Katia was gone by the time I woke up, but what she left us with was an insatiable sense of sexual adventure.

Since then we've bedded men, women and couples—only while traveling, never back home. Today will be a first, though, and I not only don't want to let you down, I'm curious what it'll be like. Though I've had more partners than most of my married friends, when I'm with you, it always feels like married sex, no matter how many people are in the room. This time, it's just me, and I have to imagine you watching, you whispering to me, you encouraging me. I still get nervous, as you well know, but I've loved every single one of our encounters, both in the moment, and how they spur us on later when we're alone.

I text you a quick hello along with a photo of me, and just as I'm finished sending it, I see a man watching me. His head is shaved, and he towers over my five-two frame. I can tell he's muscular from how his suit doesn't quite fit him, even though he looks amazing. He's taller and wider and probably stronger than you, but again, I know that if you were here you wouldn't be threatened. Remember that pro football player we picked up, the one who not only bent me over and, with my head buried in the sheets, fucked me so well I squirted, but also fucked you?

I think about that when I'm alone sometimes. It was one of the hottest things we've ever done. I wonder if Mr. Muscles would ever want to be with a man like you. Instantly, I blush; I can never hide that.

You've told me that's one of the things you love about me—how easily I blush, how readily you can tell when I'm thinking something dirty. The muscle guy walks over. "Hi," he says, his voice deep yet somehow boyish. "You busy?"

"Just waiting for my plane. Going on a business trip," I say.

"Me too. Meetings, but not till three tomorrow." Our flight's at seven and is only an hour and a half, which means we both have a whole night free. "Look, I don't want to bother you if you aren't interested"—he nods at my wedding ring, which I only take off when I shower—"but I couldn't help noticing you."

"I'm interested," I say quietly. I've had this conversation dozens of times, but it's never easy to tell a stranger you're in an open marriage, and it's even more challenging without you by my side to help ease things along. "I'm…available. Tonight, anyway," I say with a laugh.

"Tonight works for me," he says. I motion to the seat next to me and we sit in companionable silence. I have an urge to lean my head on his shoulder, so I do. He strokes my hair, a seemingly gentle touch, but one that sends shivers running through my body. I picture you on my other side, and me snug between two men, one who sets me on edge and one who makes me feel safe—and sexy too. That's what you do, if you didn't know; I feel like I could take on the world in every way, knowing you're there for me.

I don't say any of this, though; it's too intimate to share with a stranger. It's just for you. I give the stranger a look after a few minutes, one of pure desire, conveyed through my lowered lashes. I don't need to talk dirty just yet; in fact, the silence makes our gaze all the more powerful. He puts his hand on my cheek, cupping my face toward him, but instead of kissing me, he runs his thumb along my lower lip, folding it back against my chin before pinching it. Tears rush to my eyes and I'm utterly lost in his touch. I still feel your silent, unspoken presence near me, but it's starting to recede just slightly—forgive me—as this man works his magic on me.

"I only need one night," he says, then pinches my lip even harder before moving it aside, reaching into his bag and pulling out a notepad and pen. "Write down how you're going to suck my cock," he whispers, his voice as prim and proper as his words are not.

If his command is meant to shock me, it fails completely. Instead, it thrills me. I picture you watching me as I write, you who know so well exactly how I suck your cock—and how I love it. I write down what I think I will do, what makes me most excited about this most intimate act, but I also know that sex is the most unpredictable act ever invented. Just when you think you know what to expect, someone or something or some emotion comes along to make you feel as giddy as a virgin again. It's like that with you, anyway, and I've given you at least a thousand blow jobs, by my estimate. My cheeks do grow hot, which means they burn red, as I write down my oral plans, passing the note to him and then looking away.

"Your husband is a lucky man," the stranger whispers in my ear as we board the plane. My nipples get so hard it's almost painful.

As luck would have it, our seats are next to each other. Once we're seated, I look out the window—toward you, my version of you. I wish you were here, not because I need you to be, but because I want you to be. I want you to smile with pride when I take him in my mouth, to tell him naughty facts about me while I swallow him whole.

I manage to make it through landing, though my panties are drenched by the end. I don't tell the man because he has to know by now. I've been tightening and releasing, taking deep breaths, alternating between thinking about him and you. "Ready?" he asks as the flight attendant tells us we are free to go.

Am I? Not exactly, but I'm ready as I'll ever be. I touch my phone in my purse and think about texting you, giving you a heads-up, letting you follow my actions vicariously. But I don't. I'm not sure why, except that maybe I'd rather tell you later and try to be in the moment. Instead, I nod and then impulsively take out the camera I'd so carefully loaded, and give it to my new lover. "Show him how lucky he is," I say with a wink. My exaggerated flirting is silly, but he rolls with it.

We're in the baggage claim area now, waiting for our luggage. I pose suggestively for the camera—for you, but also for this man, who, when the conveyer belt starts to rumble, pulls me close and gives me a deep, sensual kiss. I can feel other passengers' eyes on me, but I don't care. I like that they have no idea what we really are to each other, no idea that my lips are right here, my body now curving toward this man, but part of me is with you. We break apart and I am hot all over. Thankfully our bags arrive shortly. I was going to take the subway, but he pulls me toward the taxi stand.

He beckons me toward him in the backseat as we're whisked toward Manhattan. He asks where I want to go and I say his hotel; my room is just for me—and you, of course. I unbutton my coat and toss my long red hair all around, grateful it's still sleek and straight after the plane ride. He takes photo after photo, which makes me want to share more of myself. I flash him my breasts in their lacy, hot-pink bra, laughing as I throw my head back.

Soon we've arrived, and I people-watch while he checks in, smiling as I ogle a six-foot-tall woman I know you'd love to bend over for. She notices me watching her, and I smile. If you were here, maybe I'd do more than that. Instead, I follow the man upstairs, aware of how hard my nipples are. He slips the key card in the door and once it's shut, says, "You've had my dick hard the whole flight. I almost jerked off in the bathroom, but I wanted to save it for you. Show me those gorgeous breasts again." I drop my coat right on the carpet and unbutton my blouse until it hangs wide open. I peel down the cups of my bra and show him my breasts. This time, the camera stays in his bag while he moves toward me, hunger on his face.

He pulls me close and sucks my nipples one at a time, using not just teeth, tongue or lips, but a combination of all three. It goes on and on and on until I want to buckle under him. When I reach for his cock, he holds me back, though. "Call him," he says, whipping out his phone. "I want him to hear you come." I freeze. This might be too much for you; it borders on being more intimate than you'd like me to be without you. Yet am I really without you if you're listening, maybe even touching yourself?

Hesitantly, I dial you. "Hey, baby," you say as I adjust the setting to speakerphone. "What's up? Where are you?"

"In a hotel room," I say. I turn around for a modicum of privacy, but I can still hear him taking off his pants. "I'm with someone I met on the plane. A man."

"Are you?" you say teasingly.

"Yes. He wanted me to call you." I pause until the silence is more unbearable than my next words. "He wants you to hear me come."

"Oh my goodness, Sunny," he says. Now the man knows my name, but I don't care because I can hear how aroused you are. "Let me talk to him."

I hand him the phone, but he adjusts the settings so I can't hear anything except "Got it," and "Will do." He puts the phone back down, and you say to me, "Be a good girl for him, baby. I'm listening."

Instead of pressure, though, all I hear is permission—to be myself, my best self, with you by proxy. He picks me up and throws me onto the bed, and in a few quick moves has my clothes off and my wrists tied above my head with my bra. I squirm, turned on in the way only bondage can make me. He fishes out the camera and snaps a photo, then says, "Spread those pretty legs for me, Sunny." I blush at his use of my name, and at exposing myself so blatantly, but I do it. "And open your eyes," he adds.

I stare back at him until he finally gets his fix then kneels next to me to show me his cock. "Your husband wants me to fuck you nice and hard, said that's what you like, so that's what I'm going to do." He gets a condom out of his bag and rolls it on while I wait for him. Normally I'd touch my clit before penetration, but I can't at the moment. He rubs the head of his cock against my clit for me, then the wetness along my slit, but when I start to thrust and urge him inside, he pulls back. "I was warned that you can be greedy," he says, pinching my clit instead. "Roll over. Now you have to wait for my cock."

No sooner have I managed to roll over, arms still bound with my bra, than he lifts me up and positions me across his lap. He spanks me hard, way harder than would normally happen the first time I'm with a new partner. You must have said something about how much I can take. The smacks are sharp and perfectly placed, my bound wrists hanging in front of me. He gives me two fingers to suck, and I am grateful for the distraction as the whacks get even harder. I whimper against his fingers, but not in protest. After a round of blows so intense they make me wonder if I need to ask for a break, he finally touches me. I'm dripping wet, so the three fingers sink inside fast.

"You were right. She responded very well to her spanking," he says to you in a loud, exaggerated voice, making me even wetter.

Then he slides the bra off my wrists, settles me on my hands and knees, ass in the air, and enters me. With only a few thrusts, I'm coming, my moans filling the air. "I love hearing you like that," you say, and I smile. Maybe this isn't so different from you watching up close and personal. "I want him to come on your tits and send me a photo. You'll do that for me, won't you?"

"Of course," I tell you. And of course, it's not just for you; I am a glutton for a man showering me with come. Yours is my favorite, but after the way this man just fucked me, I am ready to feel him give it to me.

He turns me over, removes the condom, and stands over me, cock in hand. He's going to make it rain down on me. "Do you want to taste it?" he asks.

"Yes," I say, panting. He strokes himself, while I stare up at him in awe. I can hear you doing the same thing. When he sinks down onto the bed next to me, his hardness mere inches from my mouth, I know it's time. I open wide, and soon he's spraying my breasts and face with his hot cream, his shout echoing in the room. We hear your frantic breathing and then the long exhale of release. The man runs his fingers from my breast up my chest and neck, pushing some of his seed into my mouth as I greedily swallow it, a little bit of extended bliss.

"Get his card, baby. Maybe next time we can all get together," you say before hanging up. Wouldn't that be wonderful?

# DRAWN BY NIC

by Heidi Champa

I flipped on the lights at the coffee shop and the first thing I saw was a purple sticky note on the cash register. My manager, Brad, must have found more fault with my cleaning techniques. Leaving passive-aggressive notes was his favorite means of communication. God forbid he actually just talk to me on the phone or even send a text. I snatched the note from its place and scanned it quickly, rolling my eyes after I finished reading. Instead of more cleaning inside, my work would have to be done outdoors. Sighing, I grabbed the utility bucket and filled it with hot water.

As I strolled outside, the sun barely visible over the horizon, I took a moment to admire the latest creation of the pervasive Nic. I'd seen his wheat-paste posters all over town. Most of them were quite good. I admired his talent and his raw, unapologetic style. Some of his posters were graphic and sexy, others pithy and mundane. Every time I saw one, I stopped and looked, snapping pictures of the ones I particularly enjoyed. And I'd spent a lot of time studying the odd little drawing of a dude in glasses that graced some of his pieces. If the portrait was accurate, the guy was pretty handsome. In a hipster kind of way.

A few months back, he fell in love with the wall of our café. I could see why. It offered a huge, unblemished white brick wall for a canvas, and at night, the partial fence from the neighboring business offered the cover he would need to work in relative peace without getting caught. The perfect scenario, really.

What Nic didn't factor in when affixing a new masterpiece to our wall was my boss making me peel the stuff off every time. I felt bad for destroying something he'd obviously put a lot of work into. But I didn't have a choice. The one time I'd left one of the pieces up all day, Brad flipped out, trying to yank it off with his bare hands when he came in for his shift. Since then, I was expected to take a putty knife to the posters as soon as humanly possible. That morning, with my hangover headache still throbbing and my shoulder aching from the last time I tore a poster down, I vowed if I ever ran into Nic, I'd kick his artistic ass.

I gazed at the face peering out of the corner of the poster. It could have been any of a dozen guys who came into the coffee shop all the time. Hell, it could have been most of the guys in town. I'd long ago given up trying to figure out who Nic was. In my current foul mood, I decided that anyone who put his own face up all over town must be have been a raging narcissist. A very cute, raging narcissist.

After dousing the poster with soapy water, I headed for the door to get my morning started, when I heard a voice.

"So you're the one who keeps taking down my stuff."

I spun around so fast it made me dizzy. In front of me, in the flesh, was Nic. My heart began to pound and not just because he scared me. His drawings didn't do him justice. The only part of himself he got right was the glasses. He was way hotter than I expected, tall and lanky, with thick dark hair. The bucket handle nearly slipped from my fingers as I found my voice. I struggled to remember that I was pissed at the guy. I cleared my throat and made sure to put an edge of annoyance into my voice.

"Boss's orders."

He grinned and dropped his supplies to the concrete with a loud clatter. Clearly, I'd interrupted his latest project. God, two in one day. Nic really didn't know when to quit.

"Does that mean if it were up to you, you'd leave them up?" he asked with a smile.

He clearly thought he was charming. I added a bit of extra sarcasm to my response.

"Yeah, because that would be less work for me. Peeling this stuff from the wall has become half my job."

He shrugged, looking at the ground. Now he was trying to play coy. With his deep-brown puppy-dog eyes, Nic pulled it off with ease. His T-shirt clung to his torso, and I had a quick nasty thought about his soft-looking lips. Damn him. He was getting more aggravating by the second.

"Sorry."

The word came out with a chuckle, his façade crumbling quickly. I balled my hand into a fist, my anger returning after being temporarily waylaid by his good looks.

"I'm so sure. Anyway, if you're planning on putting up another masterpiece, could you at least wait a few days? My nails are getting ruined from the wheat paste."

He moved closer and shocked me by grabbing my wrist. Nic pulled my hand close to his face. After examining my nails for a second, he dropped my hand with a smirk, the heat of his fingers still on my skin.

"They look okay to me. Besides, if you use a metal scraper, that works better."

I pulled my trusty one out of my pocket and showed it to him. His last poster was still stuck to the blade.

"I've found that to be true," I said with a smile.

He retreated a step, kicking at a loose rock on the ground.

"So does that mean you're not going to let me hang my new

piece? They were supposed to be a set, but I forgot this one at home last night. I didn't realize you'd get to this one so quickly."

He gestured toward the rolled up poster that sat on the ground next to his bucket. The one that was already on the wall had started to peel after its dowsing.

"Look, I appreciate you wanting to complete your artistic vision and all that, but if I don't take it down, my boss will give me a bunch of shit. And I'm really not in the mood for that."

Nic smiled, moving back into my space.

"You could always tell him you did take it down and that I'm just so clever, I managed to put it back up again while you were busy inside."

His smile should have infuriated me, but it didn't. It made me hot instead. I couldn't resist flirting a little more.

"You think you're that clever, huh?"

He nodded, inching us both closer to the wall. When my back hit the bricks, he leaned down and spoke right next to my ear.

"I do."

"I'm sure," I said with a smile.

His hand rested on my shoulder, the pad of his thumb rough with paste and paper.

"Or maybe there's another way I could convince you to let me put up the poster."

I should have pushed him aside and gone into the café. But, I didn't. I didn't want to.

"You really think you're cute, don't you? I mean, that's why you put your picture on your posters."

He smirked at me, the smell of his cologne mixing with the coffee smell that was always on my clothes.

"Oh, I don't think I'm cute. But I'm pretty sure you do."

"I think you're an arrogant prick who makes my life harder with his silly drawings."

He laughed, his lips hovering a few inches from mine.

"Yeah, but you think I'm cute too, right?"

Before I could answer, he kissed me, his whole body pressed to mine. When he pulled back, my eyes darted to the street. Only a few cars had trickled by as it was still far too early for rush hour, but our position was still too exposed for my liking. Grabbing a handful of his paste-splattered shirt, I dragged him toward the back of the building, giving us a bit more privacy. I was shocked when he spoke up.

"Aren't you afraid someone will see us?"

I chuckled, yanking his T-shirt up so I could get a look at his body.

"You're not serious? Don't tell me the famous Nic is afraid of getting caught?"

His confidence returned quickly as he reached for the hem of my coffee-stained work shirt.

"Getting caught for what we're about to do is a little more serious than getting caught putting up a poster," he said in a whisper.

I grinned as I ran my hand down his chest, the dark hair there soft and silky. Using the fabric of his jeans to pull him close, I looked him dead in the eye.

"Then we better not get caught."

"I think we can manage that."

He pushed me back against the wall, kissing me hard as his hands stole under my shirt. His nimble fingers teased me through the lace fabric of my bra, my nipples turning to tight peaks. Nic's mouth dropped to my neck, my back arching away from the bricks at the feeling of it all. The silence of the morning was broken by the bark of a dog. Out of the corner of my eye, I saw a beagle and his owner walk past. Nic didn't even pause for a moment, his nerves clearly more honed than mine.

Nic flicked open the front clasp of my bra with ease; the touch of his palms against my skin made me jump. When his thumbs strafed over my most sensitive flesh, I gasped and moaned. After another kiss, he whispered in my ear.

"You might want to be a bit quieter."

I opened my mouth to give him a smart-assed reply, but I didn't get the chance because he pulled my shirt up, the cool morning air hitting me right before the heat of his mouth did. My fingers twined through his hair as each sucking pull on my nipple turned my insides to mush. Try as I might to be quiet, it was too difficult to keep the sounds of pleasure from coming out of my mouth. He paused for a moment, long enough to look at me before resuming his torture of my hard nipples with his hands and mouth. I could do nothing but lean on the wall and let him do it, drawing me closer and closer to losing my mind. Then, he started sinking lower, his mouth kissing down my stomach until I was trembling under his lips. One of his hands went slowly up my thigh, moving under my skirt until he was inches from my panties.

"Nic, we can't."

"Why not?"

His hand rubbed my leg, his eyes fixed on mine. A pair of joggers picked that moment to gambol by, the sound of their jingling keys mixing with the thudding of their feet.

"Because we can't."

He smirked as his touch eased closer to my pussy, but retreated quickly.

"Now who's afraid?" he asked with a chuckle.

"I'm not scared. It's just..."

My words trailed off as the lightest pressure of his fingertip settled over my clit. I pushed my hips forward, trying to increase the pressure, but Nic backed off, keeping it the barest of touches. I tried to urge him on, let him know I wanted more. I wanted my panties off; I wanted his mouth on me. But he kept doing exactly the same thing, moving his finger in a tiny circle, the force just enough to drive me crazy.

Finally, after he'd had enough fun, he hooked his fingers through the waistband of my panties, and pulled the flimsy fabric down slowly until my thong was gone. Nic didn't go right for my now bare flesh. He stood up, kissing me deep. His long fingers dug into my hips, pulling me close. My hands cradled his face, as I tried to hold on to the moment for as long as I could. I brought my finger closer to his mouth, and he caught it between his lips, sucking it into the heat of his mouth. Nic then kissed down my neck, every inch of my skin alive from his touch.

My skirt fluttered in the breeze as he slipped his hand under it, his touch finding my slick pussy lips. Our lips met as he slid over my clit, my hands clutching his shoulders for support. He went back to tracing small circles; this time the sensation was so intense, I started to shake. When he eased a finger inside me, I pulled my lips from his, gasping for air. His palm grazed my clit and I let my eyes flutter closed, ignoring the world that was going on all around us.

"Look at me."

His voice was nearly a growl, making it impossible to disobey. When I blinked my lids open, I was met with his stare, intense and strong. Nic gave me a quick kiss before dropping to his knees in front of me. Nic eased my legs wider still and pushed my skirt aside. I gasped when his tongue squirmed over my clit for the first time, and grabbed a handful of his dark hair. Cars started to stream past the café at a steady rate, the sun finally rising over the horizon.

I felt his finger slip inside me, then another. They moved in and out in a steady rhythm, my pussy clutching with each thrust. His tongue traced undetectable patterns over my clit, making it impossible to choke back my moans. Peals of laughter echoed off the building, but the last thing on my mind was getting caught. All I could focus on was the feeling of Nic's mouth and hands. The tension in my body started building, my legs shaking, my back scratching and sliding against the brick wall. I eased my grip on his hair, but kept my hand in place, afraid to let go for fear of falling.

When Nic sucked my clit between his lips, my composure melted away and I was coming, my pussy clenching tight around his long fingers. I wanted to scream out, but somehow managed to keep the sound to a low roar, my whole body shaking as the pleasure racked through me. Nic didn't let up, wringing every last bit of ecstasy out of me, until I could barely stand. He stood as I struggled to catch my breath, my eyes hazy and blurry. I wasn't expecting him to kiss me, but I was glad he did. As soon as my body would cooperate, I straightened up and rehooked my bra. Nic handed me my panties with a sly smile and even pretended to be engrossed by his bucket while I slipped them on.

"Go ahead and finish the piece. I'll let it stay until this afternoon. After that, well, I can't make any promises. My boss will most likely tear it to shreds."

He chuckled and wrapped his arms around me.

"It's okay, I'm used to it."

He kissed me again, his lips sweet and tender.

"When you're done, you should come in and grab a latte or something. We don't open for a while yet," I said with a smirk.

He picked up his poster and smiled.

"Thanks, I will."

I waited, but Nic never came into the café. I walked outside, just before I was set to open to check out his new poster. But my attention was stolen by a piece of paper he'd pasted to the back of the door. Staring up from the corner of the page was a drawing of Nic, his eyebrows furrowed, a question mark in a bubble over his head. His phone number was scrawled in thick black letters. I smiled as I started to peel the paper away.

Damn, he really was an arrogant prick.

# THE ROPES

by Elise King

A bald man waited at the baggage claim, holding a maroon and white sign with the Affinity logo. He found my name on his list, then he took my bag and directed me outside to a shuttle bus with its doors wide open. I had no idea what to expect. My boss had suggested I go into the training with an open mind, so I resisted my urge to do an internet search and find out exactly what it was about. All I knew was that my company required the Affinity training in order to be considered for any management position, and I had a good shot at the promotion I wanted once I got through this class.

The people on the bus were at least ten years older than I was. One woman scowled, clearly sizing me up as I walked past her. I found a seat toward the middle and waited quietly until the driver returned.

The drive was about an hour. Once we got out of Denver, we took a long, winding road up the side of a mountain. My ears popped as we drove farther and farther up the mountain. At last we reached a building that resembled an oversized log cabin. Stepping off the bus, I was struck by the cool air and the fresh scent of evergreen. Several people stood outside, all of them wearing the same maroon T-shirt as me. I joined the group just as a woman came out of the cabin and stomped toward us. "My name is Julie," she shouted. "Welcome to Leadership Development. These next two days are going to be jam-packed, so let's get started. Find a partner and introduce yourself."

I glanced around the group, but couldn't make eye contact with anyone. I walked toward a younger woman who was standing by herself, but another man got there first. Alone in the middle of the group, I realized everyone had a partner but me.

"Everyone have their partner?" Julie asked.

"I don't have one," I said.

"What?" She scanned the group, counting bodies, and ended with nineteen. "Somebody's missing—" She looked angry for a moment and then shook her head. "We're already behind schedule so I'll be your partner."

I walked over to Julie and noticed she was shorter than me. But what she lacked in height, she made up for in muscle. Even her walk reminded me of the strut of a bodybuilder at the gym, moving from one machine to another. "This way," she commanded, and we followed her around the cabin where there was a trail leading through the trees. At the end of the trail, my heart skipped—and then it started beating ferociously.

In the clearing I saw an enormous structure. It was made mostly of wood with a few sections of rope. I had to squint away the afternoon sun to really see it. Most of it was probably thirty feet off the ground. Right above the first dizzying level, there was a higher one, maybe fifty feet up. There were a series of wooden perches, each separated by some type of apparatus made from wooden beams—or just ropes.

Back in the third grade, Brianna Mulligan dared me to climb up the outside of the school jungle gym. I remember looking down from the poles just before I reached the top. Seeing how small the kids on the ground looked gave me a sick ache in the pit of my belly.

I had that same feeling now.

Julie thrust harnesses into our hands and demonstrated how to step into them and fasten them around our abdomens. My hands were shaking but I pulled the nylon straps through my legs and struggled with the buckle, making sure to do it just the way Julie did.

"Okay, partner, let's go up to the first level together to show everyone how it's done."

I started freaking out. Not only did I have to face my biggest fear, but I had to do it in front of a crowd of strangers. Mentally, I cursed my boss and his promises that this training would be transformative—even fun. I considered refusing, until I remembered how much I wanted to move up at work. My thirtieth birthday was a month away, and it was time to take charge of my career. I had to do this. Julie fastened another metal ring into my harness. Behind her, two guys held the ropes that were going to hoist us up to the structure.

Julie was about to give the okay to start pulling, but she was interrupted by a late arrival. A man walked toward us. Even in the distance, I could see he was strong and moved with the grace of an athlete. He had joined the group before I could catch a glimpse of his face. When I did, I recognized him immediately.

Ryan Brackett used to work in the same office as me before he took a job in our company's San Francisco location. Not only was his body an impressive specimen of long, lean muscle, but his face was pure perfection. His smooth chocolate skin and deep-brown eyes made it impossible to speak when he looked at you. He'd been the topic of discussion many times at the bar among me and my female coworkers.

Julie pointed at Ryan. "You're with him now." She motioned to the rope handlers who tugged, lifting her off the ground. My nerves were frazzled at the thought of partnering with Ryan—in addition to the terrifying climb I was about to do. I felt my knees wobble when I walked over to him.

"Hi," I stammered. "I guess we're supposed to be partners."

"Hey, Sarah. How've you been?"

Warmth spread through my chest. Not only did he recognize me, but he remembered my name. I turned my eyes back to Julie and watched her jump across a gap between two wooden planks. She executed the maneuver flawlessly and then tumbled backward. The rope handler held her weight, easing her to the ground.

"See?" she shouted. "Easy!"

I took a deep breath.

She pointed to a rope wall at the end of the structure. "First you'll climb the ropes to get to the top perch, where you'll clip your harness to one of the ropes dangling from the top, using the lobster clip." Then she showed us how to fasten the clip and how to unfasten it to change ropes at the end of each obstacle. "The most important part of this drill is not only to get across, but to work with your partner. This course is impossible to get through alone. Remember that."

My heart was a frantic drumbeat in my chest.

"First rule," Julie shouted. "If you come to class late, you have to go first." She looked at Ryan and me. "You're up."

I followed Ryan to the ropes and tried to keep up with him. He made it to the top effortlessly and hoisted himself up to the perch.

"Come on, Sarah. You got this," he called down to me.

My weight worked against the slack in the rope wall so I had to summon all my strength to get to the top. Alone I couldn't have done it, but with him looking down, I pushed myself harder. Finally I crawled up to the perch and Ryan secured us to the overhead ropes. Ahead was a narrow wooden beam that led to the next perch.

"Do you want to lead?" Ryan asked.

I stared wide-eyed at the narrow beam. "I don't know if I can do this."

"Just follow me." He stepped onto the beam and stretched his hand out to me.

I grabbed his hand and felt myself being led to the beam.

"Don't look down," he said. He walked backward so we were face to face and flashed me a smile. "Look at me. You can do this."

At that moment, staring into his eyes was less terrifying than acknowledging that my feet were moving along a three-inch beam of wood. I gripped his hand and moved with him. There was a dull screech as the ropes attached to our harnesses dragged along the thin wire overhead. Gazing at his gorgeous face propelled me forward.

"You're doing great. Just keep coming, Sarah."

Finally we reached the second perch and Ryan switched us to the next set of ropes. With his help, I made it through a few more obstacles. One required us to jump across gaps in a series of boards. Another was made of three ropes pulled tight and running parallel to each other. I did okay until we got to the fourth obstacle.

The fourth obstacle had more wood beams, strung together with rope. Ryan stepped out first and the board slid down the ropes under the force of his body weight. It caught him off guard and by the time he'd steadied himself, there was a massive gap between me on the perch and him on the beam. We should have stepped out together.

"I can't do this," I said. The ropes were too shaky to walk across.

"You have to jump," Ryan said.

"I can't."

He had one hand on the rope that stretched from the overhead wire to his harness. His other arm was reaching back to me. "I'll catch you, I promise."

The rope that anchored me had a little slack. If I fell, I wouldn't fall far, but I would be stuck—dangling in the air, helplessly. I had to jump.

"Come on, Sarah," he coaxed.

I leaned forward and pushed off, focusing only on him. As promised, he caught me, wrapping his free arm around my waist. But the force of my landing left the board beneath us unstable. I had to grip him with both arms. Our bodies were clasped together, and we were struggling to get our balance. There was no space between us. My breasts were pressed against his chest, and I could smell the citrus of his cologne. Once we were finally steady, I tilted my head back a little and looked at his face. He made no move to release me. For a second, I was sure I spotted a trace of arousal in his expression. His gaze bore deep into mine like he was going to kiss me. I closed my eyes... and then I felt him pull away. As we moved through the last two obstacles, the idea of him kissing me became ridiculous. Could a guy like Ryan actually be attracted to me? I moved through the rest of the course in a daze. All I could think about was the heat between our bodies when he held me—and that look.

*Did he feel it too?*

Back on the ground, I decided that I'd imagined everything. Instead of talking to me, Ryan stood with a group of guys who'd finished the obstacle course after us, making small talk. At dinner, when he sat at a different table, I started to really feel self-conscious. Had I crossed the line with the way I held onto him? Maybe the look he gave me was really one of rejection.

I wanted to run away and hide.

After dinner we got our roommate assignments. Mine was Carol, the woman who'd glared at me on the bus. "I hope you don't snore," she said. "I'm a light sleeper."

"I don't think I do."

I changed for bed but I couldn't fall asleep. So once Carol started to snore, I grabbed my jacket and snuck out of the room.

I walked out to a bench behind the cabin. It was dark so I took out my cell phone and started looking at email. After a few minutes, a deep voice startled me from the darkness.

"Sarah?"

I jumped and then turned my phone so I could see who was in front of me.

"I was about to go for a walk," Ryan said. "Want to join me?"

"Isn't it too dark?"

"No. There are lights on the trail."

I followed him into the darkness.

Once we reached the trail, the trees were illuminated by the faint lights scattered along the path. I could see Ryan's outline, but his face was darkened by the shadows.

"Hey," he said. "I wanted to apologize."

"Apologize?"

"I should have known that we needed to step out to that moving board together. I put you in a bad place having to jump like that. I feel like a jerk."

"Don't worry about it," I said.

We walked in silence for a few minutes until we reached the end of the trail and the dreaded obstacle course. Seeing it in the moonlight and knowing I didn't have to go up there made me feel at ease.

"Actually," I said to Ryan. "I thought I'd made you uncomfortable up there."

"Why?"

"I held on to you pretty tight."

He laughed. "I have no problem with you holding on to me."

We stopped walking right at the bottom of the rope wall.

"I was terrified," I admitted.

"I know." He rested both hands on my shoulders and dragged them slowly down the length of my arms. Standing close like that, I could see his face in the moonlight. We stared into each other's eyes and then he moved his hands to my waist to pull me closer. His body felt so warm. I tilted my head, and he brought his lips to mine.

The kiss started soft, but it quickly turned frantic. I wrapped my arms around him and held his body the same way I did when we were thirty feet off the ground. When he pulled away, it was to unzip my jacket. Underneath I was wearing only a T-shirt, no bra. He took my jacket off and slid his hands up to my bare breasts. My nipples were hard from the breeze, and his rough fingertips rubbed and squeezed them. Feeling his hands on my bare skin, I started breathing heavier. I moved my hands inside his shirt.

Ryan's body was rock hard. I started on his chiseled stomach and caressed him up to his strong chest. Heat emanated from his skin as I explored every inch of his muscular upper body.

He stopped touching me to strip away our shirts. When we kissed again, our bare chests were pressed together. I felt myself getting wet. My breathing became long and slow. I wanted him like crazy.

"Come here," he whispered and turned to the rope wall. He climbed about two-thirds of the way up and flipped around so he was laying on the ropes, anchoring himself with his feet.

"No way," I shouted up to him. "I hate heights."

"But, Sarah," he called. "I want you."

Still dizzy with desire, I started to climb. I was only wearing shorts, and the cool night air made me shiver. And yet the thought of reaching him was too appealing to stop. I climbed to him, and then he pulled down my shorts and underwear. I let them slide down my legs and shook them free, letting them tumble to the ground. We didn't need to talk. All my attention was on him and the ropes—there was no room for words.

He rolled me over on my back. I gripped the ropes above me with both hands, and pressed my feet against the ropes below. It was too dark to see how high I was, but I trusted him completely.

I knew he wouldn't let me fall. He moved down the ropes until his head was between my legs. He started at my knee and kissed my inner thigh. Up one leg and down the other. Very slowly. By the time he reached my other knee, my legs were spread wide, and I was aching for him. He put his face between my legs. His tongue slid over my lips, parting them and plunging inside. Then his mouth was wrapped around my clit and he sucked it gently, teasing me.

I moaned. "I want you so bad."

He climbed up again so he was on top of me. I felt the bulge of his crotch over my dripping pussy, and I dug my feet into the ropes to free my hands. He stopped me before I could pull down his shorts and reached into his pocket for a condom. As I slid his shorts away, he held onto the ropes with one arm while tearing the condom open with his teeth and then unrolling it over his massive erection. Every movement of his was controlled. He kicked off his shorts and kissed my neck, making me wait before he finally slid inside.

He pushed his cock into me slowly, and I felt like I was in a dream. The most beautiful man I had ever seen was fucking me. I moaned again. Reaching up to hold the ropes, I arched my back to force him in deeper. As I did that, the ropes burned into my flesh. Ryan moved faster, and my pain became more intense. Instead of moving away from it, I arched myself further. My hands were raw from gripping the ropes. Somehow all the pain made every sensation more extreme, even the feel of him moving in and out of me. My whole body was electrified.

The slack of the rope wall echoed his movements. Suspended high in the air, I felt weightless as our bodies rose together and then sunk back into the ropes. I wrapped my legs around him and closed my eyes. The fiery sensation started inside my pussy and kept building until it rocked my whole body. I cried out when I came. My orgasm was harder and longer than any I'd felt before. My body shuddered, which sent him over the top. His motion stopped but the ropes kept quivering beneath us as he groaned into my ear. After he came, he tucked his head against mine and we stayed like that, both trying to catch our breath.

"Still afraid of heights?" he whispered.

"Umm…maybe not as much."

He lifted his head to look at me. "Good." He smiled. "Because you know tomorrow they're going to make us do the top level."

I felt a knot inside my stomach.

He kissed my ear and whispered, "Don't be scared, Sarah. I'll be right beside you."

I looked up at the highest ropes and my nerves slipped away, replaced by something even more powerful. With him by my side, I knew I had nothing to worry about.

# STARSTRUCK

by Lazuli Jones

*Oh God, he's as gorgeous as he ever was.*

The banner hanging above the table was displaying a half-body shot of Tecton, the ebony-skinned superhero who made frequent visits to my young-adult fantasies. In the shot, Tecton wore his muscle-hugging gold costume, the spandex riddled with rocky patterns. His hair was styled into small dreads. From the center of a thin gold mask, Tecton's sharp black eyes stared down. His gaze was stern, but gentle. Sharp, but soothing.

The shot was from 1993; I recognized it because I'd had the same picture cut out from a magazine and taped to my bedroom mirror. I'd stare at it until I got hot and weak in the knees and carefully took the picture down to bring to bed with me. How else was a nerdy black girl going to get her sexy kicks in the Nineties?

Tecton was all muscle and deep rumbling voice but *god*, the whole premise of his character was that he was a gentle giant. By day, he was Tyrell Jackson, a construction worker with a secret identity. By night, he was part of the titular *Elemental Heroes*, a six-person superhero team. And, in real life, he was Desmond Kyle, the well-built and deep-voiced hunk who hadn't acted much since the nineties. Being typecast was a stroke of bad luck.

Beneath the banner, twenty years older but still radiating sex, Desmond Kyle sat in a muted scarlet dress shirt and smiled and shook hands and signed autographs. The dreads of his youth had been replaced with a short cut, streaked with silver. I stood four people away, holding a glossy eight-by-ten of Desmond and trying to look chill, though my heart was pounding like Tyrell Jackson's jackhammer. I was surprised to see how short the line was; the only people ahead of me were chunky, nerdy boys. I was the only woman in line. I was the only black person in line.

I was the only person above age forty in line.

Did I care? Oh hell no. This was the first time in years Desmond Kyle was making a Comic-Con appearance, and I was going to meet him. I was going to talk to him, shake his hand, get him to remember me.

The line moved and the guy in front of me, a tall, skinny twenty-something, handed the smiling Desmond a magazine and asked for a dedication. I watched Desmond's large hand and supple fingers glide his signature across the magazine cover.

I'd dreamt about those hands. I used to imagine Tecton crushing my ass in those huge hands, lifting me up and pressing me against a wall. He'd be just back from a rescue mission, still in his costume and mask, sweaty, blood pumping. He'd kiss me, and it would taste like salt and earth.

I'd imagined those huge hands cupping my pussy, ripping my panties off, finger-fucking me deep inside while I screamed his name. I would come so hard that I'd rip the spandex from his shoulders. "*You're a goddess,*" he'd tell me while I tore the rest of his costume off, stroking his bobbing cock and holding on to his shoulders while I impaled myself.

He'd hold me by the hips with his huge hands—he was just that strong—and bring me down hard, making me scream and thrash and come again and again. And then he would lift me up using his strong hands, bend me over the bed, and plunge his big, rock-solid cock inside me until I came another half-dozen times.

I was nineteen and still a virgin, with a tenuous grasp of how sex actually worked. But it was still a hell of a fantasy.

Back in the real world, I was still standing a few feet away when Desmond looked me straight in the eye and beckoned me to come to him. The moment he smiled at me, I forgot my carefully rehearsed spiel and stumbled forward, holding out the glossy photo of him like a giddy pre-teen.

"Well hello," Desmond said. His voice was like velvet smoke. "What's your name?"

*I used to masturbate to pictures of you.*

"Angela," I blurted. I'd practiced looking poised and sexy—I'd even worn a classy little black dress with my vintage *Elemental Heroes* necklace—but now I felt like a babbling fool. "I love you! In the show, I mean. I loved Tecton."

"Thank you, Angela," he said. The way he said my name made me flush from head to belly. I was a funny combination of nervous and aroused. I was *nervroused.* "It's great to meet a real fan from back in the day. What was your favorite episode?"

*I spent my early adulthood thinking about your cock.*

"Oh, you know!" I said dumbly. I could smell his cologne from across the table; it was earthy and spicy, exactly how I'd imagined him smelling. The frantic hammering in my chest turned into a pulsing want deep between my legs. "I loved everything you did. Just...everything!"

His large fingers wrapped around the Sharpie as he signed the photo I'd handed him. I imagined what those hands would feel like wrapped around my arms, my legs. One of Tecton's powers was super strength; Desmond looked like pure muscle poured into a gentle, relaxed frame. Like he could break you, but he'd rather cuddle.

"It was very nice meeting you, Angela," Desmond said. He handed me back the signed photo; I'd planned all along to shake his hand, but I only smiled when our fingertips brushed.

*You gave me the best imaginary orgasms of my life.*

I walked away from the table. And just like that, the liquid heat pulsing in my veins and between my legs grew cold. I hugged the photo to my chest, shivering as I squeezed my breasts together, feeling like a fool now in my sad little black dress and my sad little pendant with the multicolored iris. I'd spent an awfully long time picking out an outfit for my drooling-moron act in front of Desmond. Suddenly, I wasn't a grown-ass, sexy, confident woman anymore. I was the dorky little thing I was back in the nineties, with my stupid box braids I never knew how to style, not like the other stylish girls, and my clothes that always fit weird on my awkward teenage body.

I needed a fucking drink.

I got lucky; the Comic-Con was taking place in a big hotel with an attached restaurant/bar. After walking around the con for another two hours to get my entry fee's worth, I decided to retreat there and drown my sorrows.

I stared at Desmond's face on the eight-by-ten, and at his cute handwriting: *To Angela. Thank you for being a true fan!*

I wondered what he thought of the nervous old chick, as the bartender served me my gin and tonic. I handed him his money but he paused.

"Hey, you like that guy?" he asked, nodding toward Desmond's photo.

"Yeah," I said, taking a sad sip. "Big fan. I saw him earlier."

"Want to see him again?" the bartender said. I frowned, and he pointed toward the back of the restaurant. "He came in and sat down a half hour ago. He's still there. By himself."

Oh fuck. I think my younger self wrote a fanfic that started like that. "Oh…I don't want to bother him. But thank you."

The bartender nodded and walked away. I jumped to my feet. What the hell. You only live once, and you only get one chance to show your idol how much you admire him. Okay, two chances in my case.

I tossed my drink back, gave the top of my dress a quick adjustment, and walked around the bar.

Desmond Kyle was there, sitting alone. He still wore his scarlet shirt, but he'd undone the top two buttons. He was casually thumbing through his smartphone as he finished a plate of pasta.

I didn't hesitate. I walked right up to his table.

"Mr. Kyle," I said. The smell of his cologne instantly brought me back to the autograph table. Arousal started to blossom in my belly, but the nerves were muted. I felt stronger and sexier here, in the soft lights and mellow jazz of the restaurant. "I hope you don't mind if I say hello."

"Why, hello," Desmond said. He turned his phone off and, to my delight, tucked it away into his pocket. I had his attention. "Angela, right?"

"I can't believe you remembered my name. You must see thousands of people."

He wiped his mouth with a cloth napkin and gestured toward the empty chair. I sat, resting my elbows on the table and leaning forward. The dress was low-cut; I happened to love my breasts, and I wasn't going to leave without showcasing them.

"You'd be surprised, actually. There aren't a million *Elemental Heroes* fan out there anymore. If people want my autograph, it's usually because they have the rest of the cast and want to collect the whole set."

I shook my head, genuinely surprised to hear that. "Not me, Desmond. I've been a fan of yours ever since the show started. I wanted to tell you that earlier, but instead I almost pissed myself."

Desmond laughed. His eyes were right on mine, soft and

black. "Seeing you in line was a breath of fresh air. "

"Oh, come on."

"I mean it. Seeing a beautiful woman ask for an autograph made my day. I love your hair, by the way."

Surprised, I touched my short kinky curls. I knew there was more than the odd grey hair in there, but I don't think he even noticed. "Do you?"

"I love a woman with an afro. There's nothing more beautiful than natural hair."

I smiled, trying to play it cool, but inside I was beaming. "Listen, Desmond... What I wanted to tell you earlier is how much it meant to me to have a good, strong, black character like Tecton on television back then. When I was young, it was a weird time to be a geek, and there weren't exactly a lot of black superheroes to idolize. So, thank you for being my hero."

He looked down. Was he suddenly shy? He sure looked like it. "That honestly means so much to hear you say that, Angela. I've barely done anything since the show. Didn't think I was ever anyone's hero."

"Are you fucking kidding me?" I laughed. On impulse, I reached for his hand. He didn't pull away; in fact, it was only when his large fingers squeezed back that I realized what I'd done. "I had the biggest crush on you. You were like my first love."

I wonder if he could feel my fingers shaking. Being here with him—relaxed, thoughtful, honest—made me an entirely different type of nervous than waiting in line for his autograph.

Desmond chuckled. "You must have been, what—five years old when *Elemental Heroes* was on?"

"I was nineteen."

He looked me up and down, and I could tell he was trying to do the math.

"Same age as you, actually."

"Hang on—you're forty-six?" I nodded. He whistled, and

his fingers travelled up my hand, rubbing little circles against the pulse point of my wrist. "Damn, girl. You are like a fine wine."

I was aching now, so incredibly hot for him. But my lust of years past had morphed; I used to get excited at the idea of Desmond Kyle, at his character and what he represented. And now that I was sitting here, I was falling for the man, for the sweetness, for the way he looked at me, for the way he smelled and held my hand.

He could have been Desmond Kyle or some random man I'd started flirting with in the restaurant; I was aching for him in a completely different way.

"Our birthdays are exactly two months apart. Is it weird that I know that? I had all the magazines with all your interviews in them."

"It's weird that you know everything interesting about me, yeah."

I gave him my cheekiest smile. "So let's even that out. What do you want to know about me?"

Lucky for us, he had a room booked upstairs in the hotel. We barely made it. By the time the door clicked shut, I'd already ripped half of his shirt off. His hand was under my dress, stroking at the soaking-wet fabric of my panties.

*"I want to know what you look like when you come."*

I'd wanted to tear his pants off in the restaurant, and again in the lobby. It was only once we'd slipped into the elevator and started kissing that I grabbed at the massive bulge in his pants, balancing on one foot so I could rub my eager pussy against him. I'd left a trail of juices on the front of his pants.

We didn't even care if anyone saw us in the hallway. He practically carried me to his door, like we were a horny young couple on their honeymoon.

Inside the room, we fell on the bed, a tangled, sweaty, moaning mess. I got his shirt off and, anticipating his next move,

I lifted my back to unsnap my bra. I loved having my breasts exposed, loved the way the sweat collected between them and made me shiver when the cold air bit. Desmond was already all over them, pulling down the top of my dress to kiss and fondle them. I was a sizable C cup, but they felt so small in his huge hands.

"God," he said. "You are so hot."

"You could have anyone you want, though."

"I want *you*."

I kissed him again while he helped me wiggle out of my dress. I crawled on the bed, panting, popping a finger into my mouth and then using it to rub my nipple while he slipped out of his pants.

Desmond stopped. He was watching me, watching as I stroked my breast and let a hand wander to the top of my trimmed pubic hair.

"I used to masturbate to pictures of you," I told him with a purr.

"Show me," he said.

I opened up wide, loving the attention. I spread my slick folds with two fingers, made damn sure he was watching, and rubbed my fingertip against my clit.

"Oh God," I said, pouring on the charm. I wiggled my hips at him and plunged two fingers deep into my pussy, moaning like a porn starlet. "Oh *Desmond...*"

Turns out he wasn't much for sitting and watching. I felt his massive hands on my legs, his tongue on the inside of my thighs. Soon his hot breath was on my pussy, then his tongue, knocking my fingers away from my clit so he could taste me. He swapped my fingers for his, filling me, stretching me, while his tongue pressed hard at my clit until I clamped his head between my thighs.

And then the bastard slowed down, lapping at my pussy lips while his fingers continued to fuck me, long and slow. He was looking at me, peeking over the top of my mound. His tongue was nowhere near my clit but I lost it then, clenching hard around his fingers and moaning like a beast.

He kissed my belly while I got my breath back, licking the salty sweat between my breasts and the dark little pebbles of my nipples.

"So," he said, giving my chin a quick little peck. "*That's what you look like.*"

I pulled him down and kissed him, tasting the salt of my pussy on his tongue. His hands were in my hair, touching it, pulling it, and I was ready for him all over again. I managed to push out a somewhat incoherent "Show me you" between kisses, and lucky for me, he understood.

Desmond had gotten his pants off earlier, but was still wearing his underwear, and presented me his rather impressive tent as he got up, rummaged around in a nearby travel bag, and pulled out a condom.

He slid his underwear off, and the cock I'd dreamed about bobbed into view. It was dark brown and deliciously thick, surprisingly similar to what I'd imagined. I sat up so I could stroke it, silky soft and rock hard, and took the condom from his hand so I could roll it on.

"Lie down," I told him, and he did as I asked, grabbing my hips just like in my fantasies as I straddled him, spreading my pussy lips over his cock and making sure he could see I was taking my sweet time.

I was about dripping by the time I let his thick head nudge at my pussy. I couldn't help opening my mouth wide, like it would help me take him all in, and he encouraged me softly by stroking my belly, rubbing his thumb on my mound.

He was in me. And then he was out, as I pushed myself up and sank down again, letting him stretch me wide and deep. One of his hands went to my breast, rolling my dark-brown nipple with his thumb. I had to force my eyes to open, to stay on him.

His mouth was open, just like mine, and he was staring at me. In all my silly little teenage fantasies, I'd never pictured him with that look; he was sweet, he was loving, he was vulnerable. And he was mine.

Orgasm took me by surprise, shaking me from head to toe. He took over while I tried to breathe through my shudders, grabbing my hips hard—ah, *this* I'd imagined, only now they weren't Tecton's hands, or his alter-ego, Tyrell Jackson's, hands. They were Desmond Kyle's hands.

He pounded his cock into me until I saw the moment he came. His mouth fell open but his eyes stayed on me, dark, sharp—starstruck.

I fell forward with his pulsing, softening cock still in me, putting my cheek against his sweaty chest and hammering heart. I wanted more, and he wanted more; I just needed a moment. I felt his hands stroking the back of my hair, the rise and fall of his chest as he sighed.

"You're my hero," Desmond said.

I smiled. I was just thinking that.

# THE ALTAR OF LAMENTED TOYS

by Jessica Taylor
for KC Taylor

I repurposed the light switches on the fading walls of our home into hooks. When I flip the switch up to the "on" position, I remember it was once effortless to illuminate the dark. I hang the medicinal herbs I forage there to dry. The lights won't turn on though. I used to adjust the thermostat from my cell phone before arriving home from the hospital, too. My whole life I was spoiled with electricity's availability. I read after sundown. Water boiled in seconds. I curated a collection of toys that plugged into outlets.

"Jax! Jax!" My husband calls me. He finds me in the walk-in closet of our bedroom, where I often sit. He holds a bunch of wildflowers and his backpack today—the one that fit a laptop.

After we survived the outbreak, Beau thought we should rename ourselves, as if we had stepped into a Mad Max movie intentionally. He sharpened Jackie into Jax. "Come on, babe!" He told me, "Get into the spirit of things! Adding an X to the end of any word makes it more badass."

I didn't come up with a name to call him. In those early days,

I couldn't let the past go: I did my hair and dressed for clinic, then stood by the door with car keys in hand staring out the window. But when we played "The New Sexting Game" (we hand wrote dirty notes on the remaining Post-Its from the junk drawer), I spelled his name "Beaux."

"I brought these for your altar," he says and hands me a purple bouquet. Beau is in his mid-forties now and I'm just a few steps behind him. Probably, I'm forty-two or forty-three. The hash marks in my notebook kept bleeding together. So I stopped trying to count. My blonde hair has a few grays, but I menstruate regularly.

"Ah, thanks. I was going to collect some new ones later."

"You were always right about this house." He leans against the doorframe of the walk-in closet in our bedroom. "It really is dark."

"Well, you'd come up with good ideas to fix that."

"*Photovoltaics* and *solar tubes*." He says the words in a sultry tone, for me.

I stand, set my hands on his chest, and leave the flowers on the floor beneath my altar.

He sways with me pressed against him. "Do you remember back in the day when we would go shopping for dishwashers or ovens or water heaters and you would get so horny?" he whispers into my ear. His breath smells like peppermint—he must've used the herbal mash I concoct for us as replacement for toothpaste.

I nod and set a hand over the denim of his crotch.

Beau slides a hand in my hair. He tugs at the roots and sucks my neck. It doesn't matter anymore if I get hickeys. When there was still a hospital for me to go to and patients for me to see, it was out of the question. We see another human maybe once or twice a month these days, though it's getting more frequent. There are more of us survivors exiting the woodwork, boldly declaring ourselves after years in confinement. Some of us made it with natural immunity, others with dumb luck.

Beau has a soft beard I've gotten used to. It was inevitable after the straight razors all grew dull, so he trims it with scissors every other day and still looks dashing for me. He has a dimple so deep on each cheek that a sweet sinkhole forms when he smiles, even with the beard. His hair is mostly brown, and he has smile lines next to his blue eyes. They've been there his whole life though, even in his baby pictures.

"I'm going out scavenging," he says.

He cups my face in his hand, kisses my forehead. "Someday you should come with me. You should look at it all. There's no shame in it."

Years later, I'm still sensitive over my failure to help the world when the pandemic erupted. I specialized in infectious diseases, and even ran a virology lab for my research year of fellowship. Those viruses were gorgeously symmetric, like little pets under my microscope. Peering down at them, it seemed like everything was in control.

Beau is able to whistle as he observes the bleached skeletons scattered about, his backpack slung over his shoulder. The heartbreaking miles of stopped and rusted-out cars from the mass exodus divide the land like a fence. I saw it from a distance once, through binoculars on top of a house I'd climbed.

"One of these days," I tell him. "I'll go with you."

"Give me something to remember you by?"

I'm already naked. I spend a lot of time that way in the summer. Less clothes for us to wash by hand, if we even have the water for it.

"I love it when you're naked. Such easy access."

"Cheese ball," I laugh.

His fingers divide my brown hair. As he strokes me, I bend at the knees and they fall open to him. He kisses me deeply, like he still doesn't know the contours of my mouth well enough after all these years. I shove my body in circles towards him, inviting him to move down.

Beau sucks at one breast first while thumbing the other. I imagine the porn we used to watch on the internet. As he smooths his wet mouth and tongue over my nipple, I see the round tits of my favorite performer. While my chest is caressed, I imagine releasing her D-cup breasts and then licking her pink nipples. I swell and flood onto Beau's hand.

"Who're you thinking about?" he asks me, muffled as he looks up from the corner of his eye. "Your tattooed Severin Graves?"

"No, I'm too old for her now," I say with my head tilted back and my throat pushed forward.

"Tabitha Stevens?"

"You loved her black hair and those big tits, too. I bet you would've loved to fuck her while she ate my pussy," I tell him.

Beau becomes serious. He grabs my chin.

"Fucking smack me," I say. His dick presses harder against my stomach.

When Beau smacks my face, it's more of a dull thump, like a slowly speeding pressure into my cheek and chin bone, similar to being spanked or having the roots of your hair tugged. He knows how to correctly execute the move. It sounds just like the muted beat of his thighs and swollen balls against my cunt. The noise of his hand on my cheek is an omen of terrific sensation to come. I'm not submissive. It's the flow of his energy to me, our mutual charge that gets me.

I hear the dull smack of his hand before I feel the slight sting. My wetness becomes obvious, as if we've been at foreplay for an hour. I move onto my knees before him with a smile, both of us swelling and hot. I undo his worn leather belt and slide his jeans to his ankles. Loudly spitting onto his dick, I look up into his eyes, the way he loves, before I take him into the back of my throat. I stroke him with one hand as I suck. With the other hand, I press my nails gently into the side of his ass.

I pull my face back and the end of his cock makes a popping

sound as it leaves my mouth. Gazing up at him, his dick rubs between my tits as I press them together to increase the friction. It's almost time. It's almost the moment to give him something to hold during the solitary days of his scavenge. He only needs to hear four small words now.

"Come on my face."

I shove my throat down onto him and it contracts like a climaxing cunt three times as I gag and he groans. He whips his dick out from my mouth and his hot semen explodes on my face while he strokes himself. After his final white pulsation, we both giggle like conspirators. He wipes my face clean.

We're next to my altar, the Altar of Lamented Toys, which will soon be decorated with the flowers my love brought. There are a few that don't require electricity. My favorite of these is a stainless steel wand with an end like the billowing crown of a cock. On the other end, three tapered bulbs. I nod my head toward it. Beau slides the solid metal slowly into my sex. Then he lays his tongue on me as he rotates the wand with patience. It feels like it takes a full minute for him to drag the toy one millimeter. One spin, I grip his shoulders. Two spins, I pull my knees into my chest. Three spins, I rub my breasts.

"Oh fuck, I'm gonna come." Another slow spin. Years ago, when I looked down at him tonguing me, I wouldn't have seen the bones of my hips like I do now. When my climax arrives, all these thoughts stop. My brain shuts the fuck up for a few seconds. After my sharp calls of "Yes! Yes! Fuck!" the world is silent, and I am suspended in it like a bird.

We curl up on the bed for a few moments before he goes. When the gunshots and looting started in the beginning of the end, we dragged this mattress into the closet and set up a collection of sharpened kitchen knives at its foot. We took those nights in shifts. I remember, now, joking about such scenarios when we'd bought the mattress years before in an ecological furniture store.

"Honey, the mattress is organic, compostable soy!" I had exclaimed.

"Sweet, we can eat it after the apocalypse."

Three days later, Beau is still gone. It's midday, the only time there's enough light in this part of the house to see. I'm starting to worry. If he's gone four days, I'll lose it. I won't know how to track him if it comes down to it. Infection isn't my concern anymore. Those days are gone. The remaining host population is too small, and probably mostly immune. It's the leftover people that concern me, the accidents that could happen.

The Altar of Lamented Toys is on a low shelf in the walk-in closet, so I can sit in front if it cross-legged to reminisce. The toys are arranged like a field of monuments. They rest on the blue velvet of a dress I cut up; when I touch it, I remember the way the lining of a fancy casket would depress beneath your hand. Woven in between the toys are dried flowers and offerings of useless coins from the old world. Brass swans flank the edges, guarding my souvenirs. There are photos of old friends and our last dog, Lucy.

Two of the vibrators are smooth, ergonomic. I preferred them during the weeks when people were first getting sick, and I did so many lumbar punctures in the hospital that I got tendinitis. At the perimeter, near the swans, there are some ancient toys kept for sentimental reasons alone. One looks like a rabbit and never got me off despite its hype. But it was the gateway vibrator. Another is dolphin shaped. It symbolizes the kitsch of that world. I never wanted to be fucked by a porpoise.

Behind the mammals begins my line of pulsators, marketed a few years before the fall. My favorite one is firm to the touch but smooth, like brushing my hand over Beau's bicep. I try not to think about his absence, the sensation of my chest caving in. The pulsator has furrows, like the crests of a series of waves cast in silicone. Even looking at it, my cunt clenches and my nipples harden. It still works in a way. It slides in and out of me slowly, each edge catching the entrance of my sex, getting me ready to be fucked hard by Beau's cock.

My favorite toy of all time looks like a copper-colored electric toothbrush. So much so that I would become aroused brushing my teeth years ago. This toy didn't vibrate, and it didn't pulsate. It plugged into the wall and oscillated your clit. Unlike my ridged pulsator, the clitoral attachments on this toy are useless now. Before we owned it, I wasn't multi-orgasmic. The first time I used it, a gift from Beau on my thirty-fifth birthday, I came three times. Eventually, I would push it to eight or nine times. Cross my heart.

"Where's my Eroscillator?" I yell. The toy isn't in the center of the altar where I've stared at it for years.

I crouch onto my hands and knees, getting closer to look for it. I start to sweat, and a tremor begins in my hands. I eye each of the other toys with suspicion.

"Where the fuck is it?" Sticking my head in and out between the vibrators, my pulse speeds.

"Where the hell could it've gone?" I cry. It isn't on the shelf next to the altar, tucked between the curing onions and garlic. I knock over jars of sorted herbs on the shelf above, but there's still nothing. Starting over, I search again through the toys on the altar. Three or four times more I do this, and the Eroscillator still isn't there. I feel defeated, stolen from. Who could've taken it but a ghost?

I walk out to the garden. There's still no sign of Beau. If he doesn't return, I'll have to climb onto the roof alone to empty the squirrel traps. Without him to pin them down, they'll stare at me when I club their heads. Would I even survive a winter without his body pressed close to mine in bed? More importantly, would I ever smile or laugh again without him?

The long grass curls between my legs and brushes my thighs as I lay down next to the garden. I look up to the sky, staring into the blueness that won't end.

* * *

I fall asleep in the grass, and wake up in the fluorescence of sundown. In the old days, I could've flipped a light switch and continued the search for the Eroscillator. Is it worth it to burn a candle and waste a match for this? From the standpoint of physical survival, it isn't. Beau could cut himself in the middle of the night and I would need the light to suture him. If he comes back. There are a handful of batteries that still carry enough charge to dimly light a flashlight. Those are for true emergencies. But there is a part of me that longs to still be alive in another way besides simply eating, staying cool, and staying warm. I used to be so much more than just survival.

The candle stash is in the basement. Dusk is so far progressed it will be a grope to find one down there. I enter the house, still and peaceful. Descending the stairs I hear a rattle, the smack of metal on metal, and the small sound of a knife slicing. I'm in the pitch black, and someone else is down there. If Beau had come home he would have seen me by the garden when he came in the side fence.

My skin rises into bumps, and my hair becomes hackles like a wolf's before it decides to go forward or retreat. Before I can decide, a slow glow glissades around the corner of the staircase. It's so beautiful, softly yellow and so easy.

Better than witnessing the electric light burning in the basement is discovering Beau bent over a car battery. I haven't seen one in so long, it seems like a cartoon. He looks up and smiles while he continues to fiddle with a copper cord, an inverter and the battery.

"Happy birthday, Jax! I love you!"

I hug him to me and breathe his body odor, like a mix of tobacco and pepper and garlic. It's a fantastic relief to smell him right now.

"Holy shit. I didn't realize," I say. "I missed you," I continue. "So much. What were you doing out there?"

"Looking for this." He nudges the battery with his toe.

"But there are cars less than a mile from here." In my few adventures out, I've seen them. "And aren't they all dead this many years out?"

"That is correct." He replies with a nod. "That's why it took me so long to find one that still had enough charge."

His hand behind my back makes a clicking noise. The vibrating sound that comes next is a slow purr, like an old electric toothbrush. My sex clenches. Beau makes a seduction of revealing the buzzing Eroscillator to me, mimicking a striptease. He ends it with, "Ta-da!"

He pulls back from my arms and sticks the pebbled attachment he's chosen onto his tongue to lubricate it with spit. But there's no need for that. He sets the oscillator on my clitoris, and I exhale as if the entire world has been on my shoulders.

In less than three minutes I've had my first orgasm while he kisses my mouth and oscillates my clit. He lays me on my back beneath the glow of the solitary light he's rigged. He pushes the toy into my hands. Its weight feels like comfort. This vain consumption of electricity should shock me with its uselessness. Instead, it transforms me.

Beau pushes his hardness into me with ease as I spread my legs for him. The Eroscillator zooms over my clitoris. Every inch of his dick pressing into me is a delight. From my head to my toes, my body feels as if it is charged with voltage, waiting to surge. Each thrust is punctuated by my vibrating clit that grows and swells. My blood is a current of waves through my body, illuminating me. My sight blurs; I'm looking through a kaleidoscope. I scream when I come again, the sounds of a woman leaving behind a destroyed world, comforted by her last friend.

# MATILDA'S SECRET

## by L. Marie Adeline

The dusty motel room near Lake Charles only had one lamp (thank God), over which I threw my thin red cardigan. But I still could make out Jesse's sculpted body as he pulled his T-shirt over his head and draped it to dry on the radiator next to my jeans. His short, cropped mess of brown hair and hazel eyes made him look like a student, but his torso was covered in tattoos, some elaborate, some crude, giving him the air of a recently released prisoner, let out on good behavior. I had wanted this, him, from the moment we met, but I wasn't feeling that familiar sense of sexual abandon kicking in. It could have been that the storm had shattered my nerves. Or because we were not strangers anymore, and feelings were leaking into places I hadn't allowed them in years.

Mostly it was the fact that I felt our age difference. And I felt it acutely. Jesse was thirty-two. I'd just turned fifty. Prior to Jesse, my interest in sex was healthy, but it had begun to slow, then naturally wane. On that strange night, while a violent storm raged on outside our rickety walls, I felt crazed with want of this young man I'd just picked up hitchhiking on Highway 10 outside of Houston—the kind I hadn't felt in a long time. But I was suddenly shy to show him.

From the bathroom Jesse yelled, "Didn't your momma tell you never to pick up hitchhikers?"

"She wasn't much for advice," I yelled back. He exited the bathroom, still brushing his teeth. He was shirtless, a towel around his lean waist. *Good God he is hot, my stray cat hitchhiker.*

I sat in the middle of the sagging bed, my arms wrapped around my bent knees, clutching a scratchy water glass that had a mouthful of warm vodka left in it. I still had my underwear on, but my sweatshirt was pulled over the top of my knees. I tried not to stare, but the bad lighting cast ripped shadows down his torso as his arm worked the brush in his mouth. He looked at me like I was the best idea he ever had, swallowed the toothpaste, and tossed the brush over his shoulder.

"Would your momma have advised you against driving from Texas to Louisiana in the middle of a hurricane?" He came toward me on the bed, looking like a panther cornering prey.

"She'd have called me crazy."

"Pulling into a shady motel..."

"Bad idea, she'd say."

His face was inches away from mine, his eyes regarding my face. I noticed the scar on his upper lip, a couple dotting his brow. I could smell the peppermint on his breath.

"Would she worry...you here alone with a mean stranger?"

"You're not mean."

He pried the glass from my fingers, finished off my vodka, and gently placed it on the nightstand.

"What would your momma think of you fucking someone you just met two hours ago on a dark highway?"

"Well, momma would have understood. Plus I can't very well make you sleep in the car."

*The rest of your clothes will have to come off, Matilda. This is not the time to be bashful. Where did this sudden shyness come from? He is bringing out fears in you that you do not want to examine.* Emotions were crowding in like enemies.

I flashed back to two hours earlier, as I watched him run toward my old, trusty Mercedes, the rain shellacking his T-shirt to his chest, his body compact like a fighter's. He told me he was hitchhiking back to Louisiana, where he was from, to start life over. Houston hadn't been good to him, he said. He had sold everything, including his car.

*You have a knack, Matilda, for finding the heartbreakers,* my old friend Carolina would say. She had long passed away, but our little venture we'd started was thriving, and that night I was returning to New Orleans from Houston after a successful recruitment trip to find new talent. This was before back taxes and financial troubles forced us to sell some of Carolina's best paintings to keep our venture afloat. This was when our little S.E.C.R.E.T. was working perfectly.

To put me at ease, the hitchhiker told me his name, Jesse, and started asking me questions: where was I from, what did I do for a living? I told him the truth, that I was an executive recruiter. I left out the part about recruiting men to execute sexual fantasies for S.E.C.R.E.T., which Carolina and I had started while Jesse was probably still in grammar school. Staying secret was the group's chief mandate, but the letters stood for Safe, Erotic, Compelling, Romantic, Ecstatic, and Transformative—key components, Carolina and I decided, to really good sex, the kind of sex every woman should have plenty of.

When we started the group, a woman looking for just sex and not love was still a little revolutionary, and most men didn't know what to do with women like us. Over the years, sex for the sake of sex had become more acceptable, but good sex was still something many women didn't know how to find. As for bringing their sexual fantasies to life, that's where we came in.

We found the women, orchestrated their sometimes simple and sometimes elaborate sex fantasies, and recruited and trained the right men to participate in them. What was in it for us? Well, for starters, because of S.E.C.R.E.T., fifty wasn't as difficult as I'd thought it would be. And though I was still enjoying the process of recruiting, I was beginning to experience a normal drop in sexual interest. Sometimes I'd pass mirrors naked and note the creased elbows, the loose upper arms, the breasts beautiful but pendulous, the slight ridge of jowls, the spots on my décolletage.

I tried to shut off the inner voice, the one that said I was no longer sexually viable. But part of me was also ready to ease up on the pleasures of the flesh and cultivate my internal life, make art, mentor other women in S.E.C.R.E.T., and age as gracefully as possible.

Then came Jesse and for the first time in my life I wished I were twenty years younger.

When Jesse asked more probing questions in that dark car, I kept it vague and light, painting a picture of a woman with varied interests, single by choice, too busy to settle down. Most of it was true, but the weather, and, frankly, his proximity, was making it hard to concentrate on the conversation. I slowed to a crawl around a washed-out bend of the blacked-out highway, a power outage darkening the path. The rain was coming faster than the wipers could slap away.

"Can I make a suggestion?" Jesse asked. "Up ahead, there's a motel. This rain is as bad as I've ever remembered it. I say we stop for the night."

When we pulled in, the parking lot was crowded with similar-minded people, all of whom, we discovered, had beat us to the vending machines, drinking all the soda pop, eating all the chips.

"The vultures got here first," Jesse said, slapping the machine, exaggerating his Cajun accent. He was funny, this cute hitch-hiker. And now my funny man was sitting next to me on the bed, gently lifting one of my hands to his mouth to suck a finger.

"You are beautiful, Matilda May," he said, his tongue swirling around my finger. "I know you're thinking otherwise. But you're wrong as the rain tonight."

"I feel...beautiful. I do. But, Jesse, I—"

"Matilda, I'm telling you, men don't see age the way you think we do."

He knew me already, knew what I was thinking.

"What do you see then, when you look at me?"

I braced for the answer as he brought his mouth to my ear.

"I see heat. I see...lushness. Is that a word? Lushness."

I nodded as he reached around behind my head and tugged the elastic holding my long red hair in a messy ponytail. It fell around my shoulders in a cascade of curls. Maybe I was too old to hold onto my tresses, but I was proud of the fact that I didn't have a lot of grey hairs to cover. I was a natural redhead, all over.

"Good. That's better. Where was I? I see a woman. A grown woman who I want to fuck, who I want to make scream. I see a strong woman who knows what she wants and can get it, but who only wants me."

His words were making me wetter than I'd been in years. He began to walk a hand under me, his fingers firmly stroking under my thighs, nudging, asking for permission to enter. His hazel eyes seemed glazed, the scar on his upper lip deeper in the shadowy room.

"Where'd you get this?" I asked, touching his lip.

"I told you I was mean."

We locked eyes and I let my knee drop open. He curled a finger under my panty elastic, found my slit and played with the outside of my pussy, coaxing out more wetness from between my lips with the back of his thick knuckle. He began to slowly finger fuck me.

"You're wet," he whispered. "You're teenager wet."

"You make me that way."

"You make me *this* way," he said, placing my hand under his towel. I could feel his erection, stiff and insistent.

*"Oh God."*

With that, his kiss was on me, firm and insistent, pressing me back down on the bed. I let my hands drift up to his hair. He stopped kissing me as his other hand tugged the sweatshirt up over my breasts, over my head, leaving my arms bound up in the shirt. His mouth found a tense nipple, and he took it between his lips. His warm tongue traced circles around each one as I arched into him.

"Look at you all tussled on this fucked up bed."

His mouth made a heated trail down my stomach, and when he closed in on my throbbing clit, he paused. I gazed down to watch him dip the tip of his hot tongue, barely touching my tight little knot, relishing the way his teasing made me squirm.

"Do you want me to make you come?"

I nodded, my knees going completely slack, my arms useless over my head. He slid a finger inside me while his wet, muscly mouth swirled around my fat clit in achingly perfect circles, stopping every once in a while to suck and nibble on my tender thighs before engulfing my pussy hungrily. The build was excruciating; he took me close to the sweet edge of orgasm only to pull back, ever fucking me with two fierce fingers. Finally, mercy, as he covered my clit with his whole, hot mouth, his perfect, talented tongue gently slashing and circling, carrying me higher and higher, closer and closer...

*"Oh god, Jesse, don't stop..."* I hissed, my hips bucking into his face. *"Yes...make me come, baby...do it..."*

My wild surrender made him moan with victory. He pressed my thighs wide open, his tongue now a hot, crazed motor. I don't know if my body came or he just detonated something in me; I had the kind of orgasm that exploded from my center out, the sound coming from my throat animal and desperate. I flung my arms down, both still twisted together in the sweatshirt. I placed my hands on the back of his damp head as his tongue lapped and pulsed, bringing me to earth, the crescendo waning, my whole body just washed ashore in a pool of sweet bliss.

"Jesse, you wrecked me," I murmured to the stained ceiling, my eyes shut. Before I could crane up to gaze at his glistening mouth, he expertly, quickly, flipped me over onto my stomach. Then he buckled my hips back into his groin, his hand pressing down on my back, pushing me into the bed. I could feel his erection prodding my lips, soaked and ready for him.

"I'm not done with you," he said, his voice choked with desire. "I'm gonna fuck you hard...so hard, I'm going to fuck the fear right out of you."

He entered me slowly, splitting me, filling me up with his hard cock. Once inside me fully, he stopped, a gentle hand on my hip, the other on my back, his thrusts tentative at first. I could feel every inch as he slid in and out, slowly, slowly, my wetness astonishing even to me.

"Look at us," he whispered, his body bending over mine, his ripped arms caging me on either side. I turned to face the scratchy mirror over the dresser, pressing my back into his stomach. "We were made to fuck each other."

*We do look hot, fucking like that.*

His tanned arms and tattooed body were animal, every thrust setting off a cascade of ripples down his lean torso. My skin glowed creamily in the scratchy mirror, my hair a tangled red mess down my sides. I arched my back into him and he took his cue to fuck me harder, the way I liked it, the way I've always liked it, his cock so fierce, so big, I never wanted it to leave my body.

I came again, which sent him into a tizzy of fucking, as my pussy clenched and pulsed with pleasure. Somehow I knew in the seconds before he came, when his breath quickened, his thrusts more insistent, that this man would change my appetites for good. The moment he came, his cock throbbing, his head thrown back, I knew I'd one day need this man. And I hated it. I wanted to want him, but he satisfied something in me that went beyond craving; he felt vital, like his red blood cells had mingled with mine the second he released in me, my name on his damp lips. I knew from then on, I'd feel wilted without him, which filled me with joy—and dread.

I said nothing about this to him, not for years.

He collapsed on the bed facing up, catching his breath, his hand resting on my ass.

"Holy Christ, Matty. Was that...how did I do?"

"You have to ask?"

He rolled up, his head on his elbow, and traced a hand down my back. He was thinking. I kept my face buried in the bed. I knew what was coming. The debrief.

"Was it better than the last go-around?" he prodded.

This was the third time we'd run through the "hitchhiker scenario," a sex fantasy that was high on the list of our latest candidate. My job was to prime Jesse to perform it to her exact specifications. This is what she said she wanted. He was what she would get, lucky girl.

"I give this run-through...an 'A.'"

He hissed, "Yes."

"You were very consistent this time. A brilliantly sexy hitchhiker, edgy but not too seedy. You asked just the right amount of questions, not too many, though I'd ease up on the job stuff. Our women want to keep their anonymity. I mean, they know you are carefully vetted by S.E.C.R.E.T., but don't get too, too familiar with them, my love."

"Right," Jesse said, storing the info in his brain. "How about the whole 'taking you from behind' thing? How did you feel about that choice? Do you think she'd like that?"

My body shuddered at the image of them in the mirror.

"Maybe face her," I said, trying to sound helpful. "I think she'll appreciate that. It's more romantic that way. It's a fantasy, after all, and she's quite beautiful."

His features darkened.

"But you like it like that, don't you."

I cupped his face, the last moment of intimacy I'd allow myself before we checked out, grabbed a bite and headed back to New Orleans. There was no storm. The roads were clear, the dusky sky indigo and calm. But we had already become great pretenders.

"I like it every way with you, Jesse."

He sat up, his back to me.

*Here we go.*

"Then why can't I have just you then, Matty? Why can't *we* just be together? Why is *this* the only way you'll be with me? *Training* me every once in a while for a fantasy that never comes through?"

"Sometimes, often times, the women of S.E.C.R.E.T., they get a little skittish, Jesse, and they change their minds. It *is* weird that that's happened twice with you."

"That's not what I asked."

He knew by now it was futile. There was a brief moment in time, two years earlier, after we'd first met at that bar in Austin, that I allowed myself to imagine us together for real. I had come from a wedding; a former S.E.C.R.E.T. candidate had married one of her fantasy men. It was sweet, but it left me feeling wistful. And there he was, sitting next to me with that grin. I extended my stay. One week, I said. I would be Jesse's lover, but after that, it would have to end. I would not risk the ridicule. An eighteen-year age difference is too much. I didn't work this hard at my independence, I told him, to throw it away on a young man, a mere crush, a fling. I told myself he was feckless, foolish, too young to know what he wanted, aware the whole time that this wasn't true of Jesse. He was none of those things. He loved me. He moved back to New Orleans just to be near me. But I had my work to do and it would always interfere. Also, he let it slip that he wanted children.

We checked out of that hotel and drove back to New Orleans in silence. A week later that fantasy, too, would be cancelled. Last minute cold feet, I told him. She didn't want to go through with it.

He sighed. I knew what was coming.

"I don't want to do this anymore. You pull me in, mess with my head, fuck me over, then give me away."

He was right. This was cruel. We parted ways, and for years I was in the clear. My heart was bruised but safe. I heard he met a girl at the pastry shop where he worked and married her. I was relieved. They had a baby, a boy named Finn, and I was genuinely happy for him. Once, I spotted them on Freret Street, a sweet trio, him pushing the stroller. I ducked into a coffee shop to avoid them. Then I heard she wasn't so nice after all, absconding with the guy who owned the shop. Next time I ran into him, he was holding Finn's four-year-old hand. I stopped to talk. The child was adorable. Irresistible even. And so it began: the dance, the pretending, the coming together, the pushing away.

I was older. But then, so was he.

He joined S.E.C.R.E.T. again, he said, only to be near me. But those next fantasies I trained him for actually happened. In fact, he did come close to liberating me again when I thought he'd fallen in love with one of our recruits, a woman I adored too, named Cassie. I supported it, encouraged it even. They made a nice couple. But, in the end, she, too, was in love with someone else. And, it turned out, so was he. I gave up the fight.

Today we walk the streets of New Orleans like any old couple. Sometimes I wear a floppy hat and dark glasses, which he teases me about, but he doesn't have translucent skin that the sun loves to burn. And I still fret a bit. But if people stare and wonder at us, well, so do I. Finn comes up to my shoulders and when I'm alone with him, some people mistake me for his grandmother and I'm okay with that. But when the two of us are together, watching Finn's soccer game in Audubon Park, Jesse's arm slung around my shoulders, or strolling the waterfront with ice cream, the setting sun at our backs, you wouldn't think we were anything but a regular old couple, one with a few more secrets, perhaps.

# SCENTS & SEXUALITY

by Doriana Chase

People coming into the bar where I work consider me an expert on a lot of topics, due to my attendance at the local community college. I went there, first of all, because I aspired to get a GED, but certain people, observing my potential, convinced me to enroll.

I'm the first one in my family to a), get a high-school diploma, and b), go to college. I'm a late bloomer to the realization of what higher education can do for a person's future, so I'm at least a good fifteen years older than the average college student. Not that you can tell by looking at me, or so I'm told. And I don't mean just by the guys having a few beers in the dim lights at the bar.

I wouldn't call myself an eavesdropper, but working behind a bar, I can't help but overhear conversations, such as this lady, name of Lucy, bragging about her new house and her gigantic yard, and how she's always been wanting some fancy garden, but I can tell she's clueless about garden design.

This is where I can come in handy, I tell her. It just so happens

I'm studying Medieval history and I can plan an authentic Medieval garden. She thinks this sounds really classy, which I knew she would, because I know the type, seeking self-affirmation through the perceived envy of others. She hires me to work as a consultant and invites me to her house the next day.

I didn't intend to divulge this reality to Lucy, but the true purpose of those gardens was to provide the means to cover up all the smells of daily Medieval life. Throughout historical times, people believed that taking a bath was unhealthy, and a garden would be convenient. A person could pick some herbs and flowers and stick their nose in them when someone who had their last bath a year ago came close.

And besides, their food was half rotten. Imagine this huntsman. He kills a deer, then drags the carcass back to his house under the hot sun. *My Lady*, he'd say when he finally gets home days later, *let's put a ton of those herbs and spices from our authentic Medieval garden on this before we eat it to help us forget about the funny smell.*

Whenever my history professor showed us slides in class, I'd interject because I'm outspoken. We'd be looking at art depicting daily historical life and I'd say, out loud, *imagine how that smells.*

Personally, I am partial to the natural scent of a man. It's sexy. But even I will admit that the Medievals took it to extremes with the never bathing and all.

The next afternoon, Lucy and I were strolling around her yard, searching for the perfect spot for her future garden, when her brother Jax, the actual digger of said garden, showed up. Jax was wearing beat-up jeans that hugged his firm rear end just right, and big, construction-worker come-fuck-me boots. He was a couple days past a close shave, and his hair was in that specific state where I couldn't decide if I wanted to reach up and gently smooth it down, or allow my fingers to idle away through it to muss it up some more.

I could feel words coming out of my mouth in a nervous tension kind of way, and I didn't know if I was making any sense. Jax had me transfixed with those molten chocolate eyes of his. I was thinking *is it hot out here or is it me?*, but it wasn't just me. Just as I was appreciating the perfect, snug fit of his T-shirt, he peeled it off and casually tossed it onto the picnic bench in the backyard. He was hair-free, tanned and toned. I got a wicked provocation to press my cheek against his damp chest, to run my tongue down his warm torso, to undo those jeans.

I was besieged with a sudden involuntary craving for all things Jax.

Eventually, I agreed to make some sketches and a plant list for the garden and send copies to them, then I said *ciao*, like the Italians do to say goodbye. When I thought no one was looking, I plucked Jax's T-shirt off the bench and stuffed it into my bag.

As soon as I got into my car, I couldn't help myself—I yanked the shirt out of my bag, buried my face in it, and inhaled. It had a divine, earthy scent that evoked sunshine and walks through the deep woods—and me being roughly fucked against a tree by Jax.

Suddenly, real life gave me a bit of a jolt when Jax, looking inquisitive, tapped on my car window. I wasn't sure if it was because he had a garden question, or if he'd witnessed me molesting his T-shirt. I rolled down the car window and told him that I intended on taking his T-shirt home with me, but that it would be nice if he were in it at the time.

Like I said, I'm outspoken.

He blinked a couple of times like he was comprehending, and a few minutes later we were inside my apartment. We didn't even make it to the bedroom. In no time at all I had him with his sweet, bare ass against the door, his jeans pulled down to those big old boots. I hadn't bothered to take off any of my own clothes, which ironically made our whole tableau feel more indecent than if we were both completely naked in bed.

I had complete access to that gloriously lovely cock of his, and cradled it in my hands in a worshipful manner. Jax arched his back as much as he could without losing his balance, and pressed his cock to my lips. He made a series of grateful little gasps as I flicked my tongue against the rim, then kissed the head sweetly. I knew he wanted more, but I was going to take my time and make him beg for it. This is another topic in which I pride myself on being an expert.

I flattened my tongue and gave the satiny smooth shaft a long, hard lick from root to tip, and was rewarded with a shudder and a soft moan from Jax. I slid my mouth over the crown and swirled my tongue around it as I slipped my hand between his legs and gently cupped his tender balls. I teased him a bit with my soft ministrations, then without warning, took all of him at once. He grunted and bucked, but I pushed on, burying my nose in the crinkly hairs of his groin. I savored his musky scent and his briny taste. I couldn't get enough of him.

The muscles in his hips dimpled as he gently rocked into me. I sucked on him, wetting him with my tongue and gliding my hand up and down the slippery shaft.

He rested his hand on my head, not pushing, but guiding me in rhythm with him. My head bobbed in unison with him in our agitated choreography. I kept on him, faster and harder. I felt his sensitive sac draw up into his body, building and building. Then came the hot pulses of his simmering release, accentuated with his cry of something like surprise. I took it all, lapping up the last frothy emissions, and then leaned into him while I just held him in my mouth as he got limp all over.

We both giggled a little as I helped to release him from his prison of jeans and boots. We finally got completely naked, made it to the bed and curled up together, convalescing. A couple of minutes later he was all over me, returning the favor. I let him move in that day.

The summation of that semester was this: days going to

school, nights working at the bar, and in between, fucking around with Jax—which didn't leave me much time to sleep or study. Sleep I had no problem doing without, but I really needed to study.

Jax brainstormed an ingenious idea. His solution involved multitasking. He ripped up one of his T-shirts and used the torn strips to blindfold me and tether me to the bed, spread-eagled, naked and squirming. He took the index cards I used for studying and asked me questions based on my notes. If I got the answer right, he'd insert my vibrator into me and give it a little jiggle as a reward. If I got the answer wrong—or even if I hesitated a tiny bit—he'd jerk it out no matter how much I implored otherwise. It was very motivational.

I'd keep one of those ties wrapped around my wrist while I took my test. Inhaling the same sexy scent that I had been familiar with while deep in study helped me to remember the answers at the time of the exam. This is an excellent example of context-dependent memory. There was an unforeseen side effect to this, though. You don't need to take a psych course to understand the principles of Pavlov. Jax rewarding me with the vibrator equals conditioning, equals me getting very horny in school, equals me going through an awful lot of batteries during exam time. Et cetera.

Near the end of the semester, while studying for finals, I started noticing a transition in my feelings for Jax. It wasn't anything he did on purpose, but there was a distinct metamorphosis in how he smelled. His scent became domesticated, like bread baking. Which is a nice cozy aroma, but definitely an anti-aphrodisiac. I wanted him to fuck me, not make sandwiches.

It was about that time that my trig study group consisted of just me and two guys who happened to be twins. We were studying at my apartment, and it wasn't long before I began to speculate—out loud—about the human scent, and whether a bloodhound, or even a person with a very discerning sense, could tell the difference between identical twins such as themselves.

One thing led to another blindfold. This time a fresh, unscented one, because of the importance of variables and controls in experiments. The blindfold may have been unnecessary due to the fact that the twins were identical, but I digress.

I intended to be thorough in my research, so I French kissed one twin, and then the other. They began to urge me on by guiding me back and forth between them, along with paying a lot of attention to some of my erogenous zones.

Our experiment was unexpectedly interrupted by the precipitous entrance of none other than Jax. I tried to explain how we were studying trig, of which triangles were a very important component, leading to the inevitable circumstance of our threesome. Jax was not in the mood for irony, and he moved out that day.

I maintained a perfect 4.0, which I hope will help with scholarships to a four-year university, but I am already looking past that. I visualize myself receiving a doctorate degree in the study of scent and desire, and how they are mixed up in the limbic system of the brain.

After all, as everyone knows, the mind is the most erotic part of the body.

# ALVIN'S NIGHT

by Elizabeth Coldwell

Until I walk out of the office and see the Bentley parked on the curb, I'd forgotten tonight was Alvin's night. It's hardly surprising that he might have slipped down my list of priorities. For the best part of the day I've been in a board meeting, making a presentation I hope will stave off the staff cuts threatening to impact my department. All I want to do now is go home, where I can curl up on the couch with a glass of wine and forget about everything. But Alvin and I have an arrangement: sacrosanct, unbreakable.

He gets out of the car as I approach, coming round to the passenger side to open the door for me. From the first time we met, I've been struck by his sense of old-fashioned courtesy. Nothing is too much trouble for him. If there'd been a puddle on the pavement, I wouldn't have been at all surprised to see him lay his coat down over it so my shoes don't get wet.

"Have you been waiting long?" I ask.

He shakes his graying head. "Only just got here. I thought I was going to be late, to be honest. The traffic's backed up as far as the Embankment. Luckily, I know a shortcut."

Alvin used to drive for a living. It's one of the few things I know about him. In his dark suit and black tie, he still resembles the chauffeur he used to be. But since he took early retirement, he's been able to forget about work and indulge his pleasures— one of which is me. We keep discussions of our backgrounds, our personal lives, to a minimum. That would make what we have seem too much like a real relationship.

"So where are we going?" I glance out of the window as Alvin pulls the car into the slow-moving queue of traffic.

"I booked a table at Rodrigo's. I know you like it there."

I nod my approval of his choice. The supper club is one of the West End's best-kept secrets, a haven for actors seeking somewhere to grab a drink after they've come off stage for the night, or for couples wanting privacy and the low-key attention offered by the venue's famously discreet waiting staff. Ideal for the scenario forming in my mind, now that I'm able to devote all of my attention to our arrangement.

Settling back in my seat, I kick off my shoes. "I've had a hell of a day. Hardly been off my feet for a minute. You wouldn't believe how good it feels to be out of these heels…"

I don't need to glance over to see how Alvin has reacted to those words. The atmosphere in the car has changed, a subtle tension seeming to thicken the air around us. I bend to rub my nylon-covered toes, emphasizing my point. Alvin lets out a little groan.

"Keep your eyes on the road," I order him. To an outsider, my tone might sound unnecessarily sharp. To Alvin, it's catnip.

He turns right before we reach the lights, heading down a narrow side street that will lead us into the heart of SoHo. While he drives, I take the opportunity to hitch my skirt up higher, allowing him to see more of my legs, clad in the cheap, flesh-colored tights Alvin loves so much. Another man might have preferred me to wear seamed stockings, constricting suspenders and the kind of underwear that works its way into the cleft of your ass like dental floss. For Alvin, the more ordinary my clothing, the greater the thrill.

"You know, I think I may have laddered these," I comment idly, making a show of inspecting a spot high up on the inside of my thigh.

"May I check them?" His voice is pathetic in its eagerness. "Once we're inside the club, I mean."

"Only if you've been very good."

"Oh, I have, madam. I promise."

*Madam.* I smile to myself. He's never called me anything else. Sometimes, I struggle to remember whether he actually knows my name.

Rodrigo's is on a quiet street just off SoHo Square. Some nights, Alvin has to drive around for ages looking for somewhere to park, but today we're in luck. A four-by-four with black-tinted windows pulls out of a metered spot just ahead of us. Alvin guides the Bentley into the freed-up space. I wait on the pavement while he pushes coin after coin into the meter, then we descend the wrought iron staircase that leads to the club's entrance together.

There's no sign above the door, just a nameplate beside it with the single word, *Rodrigo's.* A bouncer in an ankle-length black overcoat stands guard to turn away rowdy and unwanted customers. When Alvin gives the man his name and the details of his booking, he lets us in with a slight nod of acknowledgement.

Inside, a handsome, blond waiter in a smart white jacket leads us to a booth just big enough for two, with a small, circular table set before a deep banquette seat. There's a piano installed in the far corner of the room, and the pianist is playing old show tunes. The color scheme here is burgundy and black with gold lamp fittings, creating an ambience that puts me in mind of a tart's boudoir. You don't need to appreciate all things camp to be a regular here, but it helps.

I choose my drink without needing to consult the menu. Rodrigo's is famous for its dirty martinis, and when Alvin and I are here, we never have anything else.

While the waiter goes to place our order, I remove my jacket. The outline of my bra will be visible through my cream blouse, and that's all it takes to ensure Alvin's attention.

"How—how are your feet?" he asks. He knows he risks my wrath by daring to raise the subject, but being in the cozy, velvet-lined interior of the club has clearly made him reckless.

"Did I give you permission to inquire?"

"No, madam, but—"

"If you must know, they're particularly hot and sticky tonight."

If I looked beneath the table, I know I'd see a substantial bulge in Alvin's neat twill trousers. It's almost laughably easy to push his buttons, his fetish is so deeply ingrained. Red-painted toenails beneath light-tan tights, court shoes, sweaty feet and an occasional flash of plain white panties. The combination is hardwired into his brain, to the extent where it's all but impossible for him to come without them. I don't ask how these things first came to turn him on; I'm just pleased that catering to his needs requires so little effort on my part.

"I can do something about that for you, madam, if you'll let me."

"Very well." I try to make it sound as though I'm allowing him to touch me under sufferance. In truth, I think Alvin's missed his calling in life. The man was born to be a masseur.

I put my left foot in his lap, making sure it rests on the swell of his cock. His breath is a tormented hiss as I apply pressure with my heel. Sometimes he begs me to do the same thing with the spikes of my stilettos, grinding them into his erection. He swears that the pain would add extra sweetness to his pleasure.

Alvin takes my foot between his hands and uses his thumbs to knead the sole. The stresses of the day begin to melt away under his assured touch, and I lean back against the banquette, my eyelids fluttering shut.

"Your martini, madam." It's not Alvin's voice but that of the waiter.

"Just set it down on the table," I tell him, too relaxed to bother opening my eyes. There's a soft clink as he does just that, then I expect to hear his footsteps walking away. When it doesn't happen, I turn my head to see him standing in the booth, his gaze fixed on Alvin's hands as they work on my foot.

"Did you want something?" I snap. Doesn't he realize this is a private moment, not intended for anyone else's eyes?

"No, I just—" he stammers.

"Could you fetch us some rice crackers?" Alvin asks. I don't know whether he actually wants something to nibble on, or if he's simply trying to defuse the situation. The waiter nods and scurries off towards the bar.

When he's gone, Alvin says, "Don't you think you were a little hard on him there, madam?"

"Not at all. He's not being paid to stand round gawping at us."

"Well, have you considered that some men like to watch?"

"Alvin, I don't want your opinion, just a foot massage."

He says nothing, but inside he'll be enjoying the thrill of being treated with such contempt. Alvin loves to be reminded that he's a worthless, inferior being, deserving of my disdain. It's not what I think of him, but it's what he needs to hear.

I take a sip of my martini, relishing the dryness of the gin and the salt tang of brine. Alvin lifts my foot to his lips. He takes my big toe in his mouth, sucking it through the thin nylon. The motion sets up an answering pull in my pussy. A pulse beats steadily there, and my juices dampen the crotch of my underwear.

"You know, I need to get more comfortable..." As I speak, I let my thighs loll as widely apart as my skirt allows. All Alvin has to do is lower his gaze and he'll be able to see all the way up to the tan gusset of my tights, sheer enough to reveal the white panties beneath.

Alvin lets my toe drop from his lips. "Oh, that's nice," he mutters.

"Less talking, more licking," I remind him.

He continues to massage my foot while he sucks each of my toes in turn. I can't imagine the thin mesh smells too fragrant, but for Alvin that's all part of the attraction. The first time he brought me here, I confessed I'd changed into fresh tights before meeting him, having ripped the old ones on the corner of my desk. The look of disappointment in his eyes is still vivid in my mind. I've never done that since.

As I thought, there's a run in the pair I'm wearing, just above the knee. I pick at it, causing the fine mesh to ladder further. Aware of Alvin's eyes on the movement of my hand, I can't resist moving it slowly, all the way up to the mound of my pussy. My middle finger comes to rest on the place where I'm hottest, wettest.

Alvin, his mouth still crammed full of my toes, makes a gulping sound. I'm sure he's desperate to touch himself, too, but that's not allowed. Only once he's back in his flat will he be able to bring himself off. That's the rule, and he's never argued with it. I think he enjoys the feeling of frustration, of wanting everything he can't have.

Made bold by the privacy the enclosed booth affords us, I pop open the top three buttons on my blouse, so the upper curves of my breasts come into view. Alvin responds to the sight by pushing a little more firmly on the sensitive place just beneath the ball of my foot, sending a fresh jolt of excitement through my body. Someone told me, a long time ago, there's a place on the inside of your leg, a couple of inches up from your ankle, where if you apply pressure hard enough, you'll come. I've never had any success in making that happen, but if anyone could find it, I reckon it'd be Alvin and his magic fingers.

"Would you like to touch me here, Alvin?" I rake my finger-nail over my clit. Even dulled by the layers of cotton and nylon, the friction is good.

He doesn't say anything but gives an almost imperceptible nod.

"How about if you had the chance to pull my tights down first? And my panties?"

I've never allowed him to take such a liberty. In all the time we've been meeting for these monthly liaisons, he's never seen me less than fully dressed.

"I bet you'd love that, wouldn't you? Being able to touch my wet, bare pussy..."

Alvin's eyes almost roll backwards in his head. The poor bastard looks like he's about to come in his pants.

"Your—er—crackers." The waiter's voice is hesitant, as though he's afraid to make his presence felt and break the moment. I wonder if he's just arrived with our order or whether he's been standing there a while, listening to me tease Alvin.

"Put the dish down," I order him.

He doesn't retreat once he's done it. Really, I should tell him to go away. He's already intruded on our scene once. But I don't. There's a part of me that likes the idea of this guy, with a nice, firm ass in his snug-fitting uniform trousers, staying to watch.

My eyes meet the waiter's. Unlike Alvin, he doesn't imme-diately look away, and there's a clear challenge in his gaze. The contrast between middle-aged, patient, obedient Alvin and this insolent young man intrigues me.

Alvin has paused in his worship of my foot. I snap my atten-tion back to him. "Did I tell you to stop?"

In response, he sucks harder on my toes. His devotion to me isn't in doubt. Alvin always does whatever I want, prepared to put my desires before his. That knowledge makes me powerful. It's my turn-on, just as the scent of my feet and the color of my toenails is Alvin's.

Again I stroke my pussy through the wet cotton of my underwear. Now two pairs of eyes are fixed on the fast back and forth motion. When I glance at the waiter, he's rubbing a hand over the front of his trousers, where the fabric is tight over his bulging cock. The pianist plays on, but the music, and the chatter of the other customers, seems to be coming from another room.

Alvin's thumb presses against the sole of my foot, a little harder than before. It's as though an electric current is shooting up my leg, connecting to the web of nerves that extend out from my clit. The circuit completed, I throw my head back, fighting not to cry out and alert everyone else in the place to what's happening as I come. And all the while, Alvin keeps kissing and licking my toes, and the waiter strokes himself, face frozen in a mask of longing.

When it's over, I'm almost too stunned to speak. Little aftershocks of pleasure shake my body, and it takes a couple of big gulps from my glass to restore my equilibrium. Alvin is grinning, strands of his hair falling into his eyes. His expression seems to say, *You wanted to put on a show, and that's what we did.*

Aloud, he says, "I think we both need another drink after that. Waiter, two more martinis, please."

The waiter bends close as he retrieves my empty glass, whispering, "You were amazing."

"Thank you. So were you," I reply, and I pull his face to mine so we can share a long, tongue-twining kiss.

That's the other thing I love about Rodrigo's. For the last three months they've been employing my darling husband, Michael, on their waiting staff. It's why I've been longing for Alvin to bring me back here, so we could play out a scene before Michael's eager eyes. And when Michael gets home at the end of his shift, I'll be sure to show him just how grateful I am that, once a month, he lets me spend a night with Alvin.

# ENTER ME

by Tabitha Rayne

Even before the crash I'd never been a fan of not hearing clearly. I tried wearing headphones to listen to music, but it made me feel claustrophobic, isolated. I get the same thing with sunglasses. I can't bear them; they make me feel like I'm in a world of my own where no one can reach me, like I'm suspended somewhere other than reality.

So that's why, since the crash, you will never see me wearing sunglasses or even a hat. Anything that cuts me off from feeling in the thick of the here and now has me panicking.

The crash left me suddenly and utterly deaf. It was the strangest sensation coming round. I felt like I was deep under-water, unable to make contact. The sound of my own voice was muffled and thick, so alien and far away I screamed. I knew I was screaming because my throat was raw and nurses in blue-cotton pajamas were smoothing their hands over me and petting me, their brows furrowed with concern.

That was over two months ago.

I still wake up with that feeling of panic. Sometimes, though,

I let myself lie in the morning stillness, trying to be as quiet as possible with shallow breaths so I know, for a little while at least, that I am choosing the silence. It is mine.

I don't know how long George and I will last. He must be sick of the bruises I inflict when he's trying to catch my attention by tapping my back. The shock! I have not been able to master the art of not being panic stricken by an unexpected touch. It's exhausting, straining to hear all day long when all there is is stifling black nothing. So disorientating. I saw a program once about a room that was so well soundproofed that there was no echo at all. When the lights were out, people could only last a few minutes before demanding to be released from the black hole. George said he thought he'd love that. He'd do anything for a bit of peace and quiet; he reckoned he'd last a good eight hours. I knew what they were feeling, though. I imagined it so keenly at the time, and now it is confirmed to me. If I close my eyes, I'm there, in that room of absolute nothing. Alone.

We've taken to notes or texting. Being unable to hear my own voice means I can't risk the words coming out. George says I sound fine. I don't believe him.

George left a note this morning.

*Let's make love. Tonight.*

I hold it between my thumb and forefinger. You wouldn't think not hearing would rob you of other senses, but it does. I can feel the paper, yes, but I can't hear the feel of the paper. Try it now, go on, rub your fingertips over the pages of a book, or a newspaper. Listen to how it feels. Now try to imagine not hearing that. See? You're surrounded. Your world is full of senses interacting and, well, making sense of everything. I begin to fold the note up, slowly creasing it into a plane. The paper is rough and crisp, and I drag my nail along the folds, making them sharp and perfect. Something about the points and lines makes a shiver run up to my solar plexus. I open the note back up and trace the words.

*Let's make love. Tonight.*

I try to savor the text without worrying how it should sound. I lift the note to my mouth and run my tongue over the letters, hoping to taste words. The shiver has become a flutter and travels gently down my abdomen and settles at my crotch. I let the sharp edges tickle my lips and the tiny hairs at the corner of my mouth. It makes me twitch and salivate. The prickle and swoosh of my breasts alerts me to my stiffening nipples, and I look down to the rise in my shirt.

It's been so long since I've felt arousal, I'm taken by surprise, guilt almost. I make a decision. We *will* make love tonight.

My lack of hearing seems to have brought with it an inability to make any sort of decision, even down to the simplest of tasks like choosing whether to wear socks or not. George says it's because my confidence has been rocked to the core. I think I agree. It's the only explanation. This decision though, this is something I need to keep and take control of. It feels precious yet strong. Like I'm on the brink of something big.

I drift the note over my nipple through my shirt. It tickles, and I yearn for more. I undo my top buttons and pull the shirt to the side, exposing my breast. I run the edge of the paper over my nipple and breathe in hard. My chest and tits rise to the exquisite feeling of being turned on. My skin is flushed and my cheeks are hot. I look around the kitchen quickly, my breath hitching just in case someone has come in without me noticing. When I'm satisfied all is clear, I go through to the bedroom and stand at the mirror at the foot of the bed.

I like what I see. I like my exposed breast hanging out of my shirt. I like the flushed pink glow over my face and chest. I like the way my fingers hold the paper which hovers over my achingly tight nipple. I like the feeling of dampness and warmth spreading though my knickers. I sit down on the end of the bed and spread my thighs. I hesitate a little, a brief moment of panic again that someone might be watching. But who?

The thought actually has me even more excited, and I open my legs further to reveal the dark stain of arousal spreading through my underwear. Pulling my panties to the side, I am amazed at the dark ruby color of my pussy lips. I don't think I've ever done this to myself before—looked in a mirror. It's like I'm not looking at me. I'm just looking at a very horny woman, and it is turning me on.

I can even smell myself now. It is a wonderful fragrance of lust and slight shame. Perhaps I should save myself for George coming home, but I know, as my pussy starts clutching and pouting, that there is no chance of that. I drop the note and reach down. There's something so deliciously naughty about knickers being pulled to the side, don't you think?

My clit is yearning for attention, but I tease it. I use two fingers in a scissor action to separate my labia. Oh, it feels good to look at my cunt, so open, so wanton. I rub my fingertips at the entrance, drawing out some of the juices, which are now beginning to trickle. It doesn't take long to coat my fingers and lips. I push two digits inside. The thrill is immense, and I twitch and spasm at this first invasion, wishing it was George's beautiful cock. I'm glistening with my own arousal, and my mouth is watering. I feel sexy-dirty, and I bring my hand up and spit on my fingers, thrusting them roughly back down and into myself.

*Oh yeah, oh yeah,* I finally give in to my clit and rub hard, alternating holding my pussy lips closed tight around it and stroking it directly. My other hand is getting crampy holding my knickers to the side so I quickly just pull them off, amazed at how raw and exposed I look without the scrap of material to hide my modesty.

I look bare. Naked. Wanton. I spread my legs vulgarly and lie back a little, sliding my now-free hand under my ass. I can still just see the action—and it is quite rude to watch my fingers reaching under and up to my pussy from behind while the other hand is busily working my clit.

My lower fingers curl into my hole, and the tensing and clutching of my pussy walls begin again. My hips are bucking, and I imagine George licking me out and thrusting his solid digits up inside me. "Oh yeah, yeah. That's it, that's it," I'd say as I peaked and fell over the edge and into the oblivion of release.

I'm breathing so hard now. My tit is still exposed, bobbing about to the rhythm of my ministrations. My nipples need attention too; I can't quite get to the brink. I can't rub hard enough. Frustration grows, and fury comes too. My lower hand is fucking me from behind hard, but not hard enough. I give up with looking in the mirror and roll onto my front, humping my bedding in furious silence. My breath is hot in the sheets and my hair is sticking to my face, obscuring my vision, so I take the chance to close my eyes and descend into complete isolation. I'm still thrusting my pelvis, and my fingers are still crammed into my pussy from behind. But it's so black and quiet. Am I floating? I resist the temptation to open my eyes and try to embrace this new world I inhabit. My pussy is oblivious to my mind's distraction, juices pouring out onto the duvet. My fingers are slippery and slide around over my clit as I press down hard, clenching my ass cheeks and trying to get as much pressure as possible.

I feel like I'm grunting; I don't know if I'm hearing it or feeling it, but it's there. I open my mouth and let the sensation of noise flood out as my cunt clenches and unclenches around my fingers.

Suddenly I am alert and back in the room. Someone is here. A hand presses in between my shoulder blades and I tense, jerking my body to throw off the intruder. I can feel the thud of my heart in my throat as well as the raspy grating of a scream.

My head is violently pulled back and a hand covers my mouth. I'm breathing chaotically through my nose, snot and tears sniveling all over the place. I am utterly terrified. My hands are scratching and gripping at my captor, but it only succeeds in my being clamped tighter in his arms. I'm writhing and jerking trying to get free, but the silence is so thick and deep I feel like I'm wading through sand. The grip releases. I fly off the bed like a wild animal and grab a hand mirror, holding it out and backing away from my attacker. I take a proper look at him.

There, on our bed, looking just as panic stricken as I feel, is George.

"Fuck, I'm sorry, I'm sorry," I see him mouth. It doesn't matter that I can't really lip read; his eyes say it all. They are red and teary.

He must see how serious it is now.

I crumple onto the bed beside him, reaching out to his hands, which intertwine with mine.

His mouth is moving but it's too fast for me to make sense of. I just shrug and shake my head.

He pulls out his notebook and writes.

*I came home early. I couldn't stop thinking about you.*

"Me too," I mouth back, patting my upper chest. My heart rate has slowed and I'm beginning to calm when I realize what he must have witnessed.

His shoulders have relaxed too.

I grab the pencil and notebook.

*How long were you there?*

A huge blush rises up my chest, throat and cheeks, and he catches my chin, lifting my gaze to meet his.

"Long enough..."

I wonder if he bothers to actually speak anymore or just makes the movements of his lips like I do.

"Are you okay?" he asks, looking so concerned, and I nod, taking the notebook again.

*Apart from being caught with my fingers up my pussy.*

He smiles broadly and I imagine his laugh. I wish I'd paid more attention to the sound of that laugh. I can hear it but not hear it. It's there, just out of reach.

*That was fucking horny*, he writes.

I look down, shirt still hanging open with my tits out. In the mirror I see my hair is plastered over my sweaty, guilty-looking face, and I'm bright red.

The bed dips and he's getting off, standing in front of me. He undoes his jeans slowly; his cock is rigid. The adrenaline-ridden air subsides and begins to charge with sexual energy as his clothes drop to the floor, leaving me with no doubt just how horny walking in on me feverishly masturbating has made him.

I lean over and inhale his musk. His heady animal scent has me salivating and hungry for release again. His skin is warm as I flick my tongue over the gloriously strained skin of his cockhead. The tiny droplet at the tip is like nectar to my taste buds. Like it's the only thing I've wanted for years. I open my mouth and gobble him up hungrily as he twists his fingers in my hair and pulls me on to him harder. I grip his hips, allowing my nails to press into his flesh as my mouth suckles and feasts at his cock. He is leaning over now, trying to catch a touch of my pussy. I shuffle properly onto all fours and arrange myself to the side so he has access from behind.

I suddenly feel detached and isolated again. Severed from reality. I need to see his face, witness this connection. It has been so long.

I pull back from his cock, and he untangles his other hand from my hair.

He seems to understand and looks right into me, smiling. He cups my face and bends to kiss me deeply and fully, while cradling me backwards onto the bed until his knees are up in between my legs. The yearning in my cunt is back, and my clit is peaking and straining for attention. I spread my legs as wide as I can and buck my hips upward in anticipation of his touch. He releases my lips and says something before disappearing down to nibble at my breasts. I writhe as my nipple tingles and rolls between his lips and teeth. He is a master of the nipple tease. But my sex is burning, craving, building. I push him downward and he obliges, looking up to give me a quick smile before diving to my desperate cunt.

He presses his palms to my inner thighs, pushing them farther apart so it is almost sore. Then he drags my pussy lips open just the way I like him to. Now he takes me. Now he falls onto me, guzzling at my swollen clit.

*Finger me. Fuck me with your fingers,* I silently beg, and he does. He rams me with two, or is it three, pummeling, plowing, thrusting until I'm clenching. But I need more.

I need his dick.

I need to be fucked.

I wriggle and curl up, reaching his head, and pull him away from my pussy.

"Fuck me," I mouth and plead.

He crawls up between my legs, hooking his shoulders behind my knees so I'm bent double. I brace myself. This position needs a little preparation. He hovers for a moment, his gaze meeting mine, the tip of his cock pressing at my entrance. I tense, and his intense expression gives way to the flicker of a smile before he spears me hard and deep, right to the hilt of his cock.

Sublime agony fills me as I stretch to accommodate him. It's the first time he's been inside since the crash, and I'm suddenly emotional. He stills and holds me there, staring at me, begging me with his eyes to allow this connection. I let out the breath I didn't know I was holding and rock my hips. He pulls out slowly and gently and my pussy walls clamp down, trying to keep him in.

Just as I think he's going to completely leave me, he plunges back in, filling and ravishing my needy pussy. Again and again he thrusts, fucking away all the distance and trauma of the past two months. It is glorious to feel so full of him, and my cunt is building and rising from deep within, as his cock pounds my G-spot. A deep internal orgasm doesn't happen often, but when it starts, I know nothing will stop the wave. My clit is welling and peaking, too, with the friction, and I let my neck relax and drop my head into the pillow, watching George's face as he fucks me, giving myself over to the sweet relief that is building.

His full weight is on me now, pressing me down, my knees almost by my ears as he plows me. My peripheral vision dims as my orgasm comes into view, rising and gushing as I slick his dick further with my fluids. His face is twisted and he's saying things now, things I wish I'd memorized better. I can feel the twitch in his cock that signifies he's about to come too.

*Yes, yes. Come.*

We need to come together.

I can feel the full length of him ramming in and out, and it pushes me higher to the brink.

One almighty thrust and we're here. At the edge. I hang in the still silence for what could be an eternity, or a flash, when suddenly I hear.

Sound, the sound of him coming fills my brain.

"Fuck yeah, baby, you're so fucking wet. I'm coming, I'm coming inside your sweet, tight cunt." The words flood my senses and I come and come, over, out and through them. Him.

"Yes, that's it, that's it. Come for me. Fucking come..." His voice is raspy and ragged as he fills me with his orgasm, and I wrap tightly around him, spasming and coming over and over again while his voice circles around in my mind.

He did it. He entered me. He entered my body and soul.

He unlocked the memory of his voice. The beautiful memory of his sound.

It comes flooding back, his laughter, his sigh, his sexy words. He always chose the perfect words to get me off. I can hear them now, in my mind. The way he wrapped his tongue around words like *cunt* and *cock*. I hear every nuance, every inflection, and sear them into my mind.

We lie together, and I cuddle into his arms and just listen. Yes, the silence is still here, but I can listen too. I filter out the nothing and concentrate on the memory of his heartbeat as I lay my head on his chest.

It could almost be real.

I close my eyes and I'm not alone.

# THE WOLF AT HIS DOOR

by Deborah Castellano

I had things I could wear for the night, of course. The Barbie-pink PVC pencil skirt I got from ASOS. The leather leggings I bought on a whim from Top Shop at Nordstrom. The gold, jingly, fuck-me Manolo Blahniks that I snaked out from under another chick during a particularly intense Neiman Marcus semi-annual. Would he even notice the amount of care I put into what I wore, anyway? Even now, he played his cards so close to his chest that unless he was being intentionally overt, I never could catch him noticing me, even though we had known each other for almost half our lives.

We had seen all of the very best and the very worst that we had to offer each other since our freshman year. We kissed each other drunk during college, we had brunches of disco fries and Taylor ham sandwiches at diners after clubbing in our twenties, we consoled each other through our divorces in our thirties, we told each other everything. And even now, late at night at a party, he would twirl me around my kitchen, and I would pretend we were in an old movie and put my head on his chest, both of us laughing. But we never fell into bed with each other, somehow.

Oh, he always flirted with me as he flirted with all of our oldest and closest friends. I teased him that he was Laurie from *Little Women* and always a little in love with all of the March sisters, which he never denied. We always tried to impress each other with stories of our debauched adventures, though they became more carefully selected as we got older. It was only a few months ago that I was regaling him with stories of a particularly ridiculous fetish event I had gone to. I was intent on checking off as many buckets on my bucket list as I could in one night since I went to events less frequently now and there were still a whole host of things I had never tried before that evening.

*I'm impressed*, he texted.

*I know, right?* I texted back. I paused a second. We were always honest with each other. *I don't know though. It was fun. It was crazy, but it wasn't meaningful.*

*What do you mean?*

*I mean, if there's no significant energy exchange, if there's no chance to get into the other person's head in a noteworthy sort of way, it's just an experience for me.*

*I know what you mean. I've been feeling that way lately too.*

*Really?*

*Yeah. I mean, it's fun. It's always fun but lately it hasn't been a very deep connection. So it can feel kind of empty at the end of the night.*

*Yes, exactly!* I thought for a moment and then typed: *Sometimes I wonder if I will ever really be someone's dominant again.* Should I have said that? Why did I even say it? None of his interests were in that arena anyway. I had begun to think none of *my* interests were even in that area, not that I had been given much of an opportunity in my travels to explore that side of the whip. Why did I suddenly care what he would think about any of that anyway?

There was a long pause.

*Sometimes I wonder if I will ever get the opportunity to be someone's submissive.*

I snapped myself back to the moment and tried to focus on getting dressed. Everything felt like a costume, like I would be spending the evening playing at being Pussy Cat Meow Meow, pro dominatrix extraordinaire. Finally I settled on a little black dress, back-seamed stockings held up with a blush-pink, embroidered-silk garter belt, a sheer black bra and gossamer black panties. I put on my black ballet shoes, feeling the elastic snap resolutely over the silk of my stockings. My hands started to tremble as I thought about the boundaries we could cross tonight, if we both could be brave. I took a deep breath and put my hands on my vanity and closed my eyes. After a moment, I resolutely put on my scarlet Nars lipstick. Cruella. Could I be? How would I even start this? I thought about my conversation with my friend Julie earlier to steady my nerves.

"I don't understand how you get so worked up sometimes, Lucy. I know, the anxiety. But you have this beast of a man who would literally let you walk all over him in heels if you batted your eyelashes up at him."

"I know. I know! I really trust him to try this with me, too. I just can't seem to get it together."

"I don't entirely understand what you're doing and it's not my thing. But you deserve a chance to see if it's *your* thing. Give yourself a chance to be centered in your power. Be present in it, okay? You've got this."

*You've got this,* I mouthed to myself in the mirror, willing it to become true as I heard his knock at my door.

We hugged hello as we always did and sat down on my sofa together as we had a hundred times before. He opened a bottle of rosé and carefully poured it into the two glasses I had put out. We clinked and sat quietly as I nervously sipped my wine while he patiently sat next to me, waiting to see what I would do.

"I don't know what I'm supposed to do," I whispered finally.

He squeezed my knee and waited until I looked into his cerulean eyes. I had never noticed before how much they reminded me of the sea. "Whatever you do, I will not judge you. No matter what. Okay?"

I nodded. I put my hand on top of his, admiring how small it looked by comparison. Delicate was not a word that was ever used to describe me, either in personality or appearance. I hissed out a half laugh. "Well, what do *you* do? You've done this as the dominant like a million times."

"I wouldn't say a million, maybe only half a million," he said, smiling. "Sometimes, this. We look at our hands until I feel sure enough to decide what to do. Sometimes everything is as carefully choreographed as an opera at the Met. It depends on the people, it depends on the energy."

"Yes, but. What do I do?" I said in exasperation.

He looked at me thoughtfully. "I don't know, Lucy. What will you do?"

I drained the rest of my glass of wine with determination. I will be fearless. I will cross this edge. I will be the wolf at his door that he is not strong enough to resist, tearing open his heart with my bare teeth and drinking his heart's blood until it fuels mine. Until his heart is mine.

I pulled his hand into mine, letting my fingernails leave tiny crescent moons on his palm, but not deep enough to draw blood. Just enough to draw a small sigh from his lips as he obeyed my silent command to follow me into my bedroom, closing the door softly behind him.

He stood quietly as I twined one of my hands into his flaxen hair, admiring how soft it was. I wound my hand tighter and tighter until my hand reached the nape of his neck, and I sharply drew his hair in my fist as his breath caught. I put my hand to his chest and delicately pressed against his chest, where I could feel his heart drumming as fiercely as a fawn's heart. Feeling him react so strongly to me sent an immediate rush of power to my brain and wetness to my pussy.

He sat down on my goose-down duvet, his hands balled to his sides. His eyes were closed and his lips were slightly parted, allowing me to stare at him freely. How had I never noticed the graceful planes of his face, the curve of his neck, in over twenty years? The newness of noticing with the familiarity of his frame caught me in the stomach, making my pulse quicken.

I straddled him, the feeling of his hardness against my pillowy thighs making me gasp. Tipping his face up with his leashed hair, his eyes were unfocused as he looked up at me. Softly, I ran my fingertips against the spiral of his ear. His breathing became more jagged as I bit the soft flesh of his ear and trailed down his neck, pulling his hair back in my fist so his neck would be more exposed to me. I inhaled against his skin, smelling the familiar, clean scent of his soap. My blood was rushing so loudly in my ears, I couldn't think clearly enough to consider anything but the feel of his hair wound around my hand and how delicious he smelled.

Trembling, I brushed my hand against his cheek and then his lips as he kissed the palm of my hand. Everything in me went limp, and I gathered up all my bravado to kiss his verdant mouth. His hands shuddered at his sides, clenching and unclenching, but never touching me. I slid my tongue into his mouth and pulled at his curls severely, his rigid cock becoming even more stiff under his grey wool trousers. I put my lips to his ear, so he could hear the softness of my whisper.

"Do you want to fuck me, boy?"

"*Yes.*"

The blood in my ears became a tidal wave. "You cannot tonight." A rush of malicious joy coursed through me. I didn't know I could be so blatantly harsh, let alone enjoy it. I was breathing fast. The fierceness of denying him swept over me.

I was so wet I could barely figure out what to do with myself. "How does that make you feel?"

He groaned softly, pressing his hardness against my thighs as he brushed his lips across my ear, sending a shudder down my spine. "It makes me want you more, Lucy."

"Do you want to feel your hands on my body?"

"Very much." His eyes were soft as meadows, and I could see he was in the hyper-present/completely absent place that submission sometimes brought, when the connection was especially electric.

"Beg me," I whispered.

"Please," he said simply. He brushed his lips against my neck, and I felt my eyes roll into the back of my head. He gently tugged at my ear with his teeth. "*Please.*"

"You may."

His big hands immediately swept to my hips, squeezing the flesh beneath my dress as I slowly writhed against his hardness, taunting him with what I would not allow him to have. He pulled me still closer to him. I licked the flesh behind his ear as he shuddered. His breathing became more rapid and his eyes drifted closed in pleasure. "Fuck," he whispered. "Fuck! God, Lucy."

The more the space between us deepened, the more I relished giving him the smallest promise that there could be a release for him and then pulling it away from him. I rolled onto the bed, pulling him by the hair to bring him next to me, but not quite touching my body, abruptly bringing any chance he had to get off to a sudden halt. He inhaled, bringing his face to my hair, and then kissed me deeply.

He did not press his suit, even though I would have had a difficult time at that point denying him—I was that desperate for him. As he continued to obey while never demanding, his mouth on mine, I felt a fine glimmer of sweat on my back. The longer he kissed me while lying so still and close to me without pushing his body up against mine, the more urgently I wanted him. Finally I couldn't stand it anymore, and I circled his wrist with my hand, bringing his hand to my pussy, pulling my panties aside as his fingers found my clit.

His hand slowly massaged my clit in lazy, unhurried circles as I arched up to better meet his touch, pulling his hair. I whispered his name in his ear as my moans became more soprano, and he drew me still closer to him, his breath warm and uneven against my neck. As I rocked against him, I could feel the muscles in my thighs becoming tighter. My head swam with unfocused desire as he steadily increased his pace. My fingers became claws as I raked his back with my nails and bit his shoulder so hard I could taste his blood in his mouth. Waves of pleasure pulsated through my pussy, making silvery sparkling lights glisten behind my eyelids. I wound my legs through his and rested on top of him. We laid entwined, and he gently kissed the inside of my hand.

When I could breathe and form thoughts again, I saw he was already giving me a soft look that spoke of more than longtime friendship. My blood rushed with emotion that was almost—but not quite—ready to be called by name.

"So, um, we're doing this?" I said softly into his ear.

He brushed the hair out of my eyes and smiled. "It certainly seems we are."

# OUT OF THE ORDINARY

by Rose P. Lethe

Margo knew the moment Alex got home that dinner had been a disaster. Not that she had really expected anything different, knowing Alex's family, but still. She winced in sympathy when the previously silent apartment filled suddenly with a series of bangs like gunshots: the front door swinging shut, Alex slamming his keys on the kitchen counter, Alex kicking off his thick-soled boots and tossing them in the pile of shoes beside the door.

By the time he reached the bedroom where Margo was reading in bed with her back against the wooden headboard, he'd gotten the frustration out of his system and was now just a husk of disappointment. His heels scuffed against the carpet, and his spine, usually perfectly straight and confident, had begun to hunch like there were heavy weights on his shoulders.

"You're in bed already?" he said. "It's barely eight."

Their cat, Harley, who had been curled up beside Margo's legs, greeted Alex with a happy *mrrw*; Margo closed her tablet case and set it aside. She didn't say that she'd been expecting Alex to come back in a foul mood, that she'd thought it would be best if she was already prepared to comfort him with a cuddle. She only threw back the covers, startling Harley, who promptly leapt off the bed and skittered away, and held out her arms in a clear invitation.

"Aw." Alex's smile was wan, but it was nevertheless a smile. "You scared him."

"*You* put him on edge, with all your banging around out there. Now hurry up and get into bed."

Alex got into bed, but not before he'd stripped out of all of his clothes aside from his chest binder, white briefs, and black socks. Then he climbed onto the mattress and crawled forward until he was sprawled on top of Margo, with his cheek resting on her tank top just below her breasts. She wrapped her arms around him, stroking back and forth over the little dip just above his ass before skimming over his binder—stark white just like his briefs, which Margo had always thought contrasted beautifully with his dark skin—and tracing the notches at the very top of his spine. He was thin and bony, all sharp lines and harsh angles—very different from Margo, who was pale and curvy, not quite fat, but certainly not skinny either.

They fit together perfectly, she had always thought.

"Do you want to talk about it?" she asked.

Alex grumbled, arching into Margo's touch. "Ugh. What's there to say? Mom called me Ally. Dad kept treating me like a stranger. Both of them still think you're some sort of horrible influence on me. Jackson said that I wasn't 'passing.'"

Margo heaved a sigh. "Your brother's a twat."

Alex laughed, although it was a harsh bark rather than the soft trill that Margo loved. "He is, yeah. And he gets worse as he gets older."

True. Margo had never been able to stand any of Alex's family, only partly because they couldn't stand her and she believed in giving as good as she got.

Alex bent his knees and brought them closer to his chest,

shifting his position until he was lying more in Margo's lap than against her chest. Margo transferred her attention to his hair, which was shorn so short it was nearly a buzz. It tickled Margo's palms as she raked her fingers through it, scratching at his scalp.

"Mmm." Alex nuzzled at her bare thigh, breathing in deeply. "But let's not talk about that. I'm tired of thinking about it. You were reading porn again, weren't you?"

Margo blinked, her hands stilling. "Erm. Well, I got to page sixty of my novel, my *mystery* novel, and no one's even died yet. So yeah, I got bored and switched to something more interesting. How the hell did you know that?"

"Because I can *smell* you." Alex dragged his nose teasingly up Margo's inner thigh until he reached her panties: a pair of solid-black boyshorts. He kissed the groin of them, right over the swell of Margo's vulva. "Mmm. You're wet. What were you reading?"

She'd forgotten about it, honestly. She didn't even feel aroused anymore, although as Alex pressed another kiss to her panties, then another and another, trailing up and down the outline of her labia, she thought that could be remedied quickly if he kept this up.

"The same thing I always read," she said. Her breathing had grown labored. "Two men having very explicit sex."

Alex nudged her legs farther apart and rolled onto his stomach between them, making a show of licking his lips. Then he hooked his fingers in the waistband of her boyshorts and inched them down her thighs. Margo eagerly lifted her hips to help.

"What sort of sex?" Alex asked. When he'd gotten her nude from the waist down, he tossed her underwear over the edge of the mattress and urged Margo to put her legs over his shoulders.

She did, although she felt awkward about it, like she was in danger of squashing Alex's head between her thick thighs. "Oh, you know. A little of everything. When you came home, one of the characters had pinned the other to the wall of a bathroom stall and was fucking him from behind."

Margo usually preferred her pubic hair shaved, but it had been over a week since she'd found the time. There was less than half an inch in growth, and the short tufts were soft and obedient, not the wiry mess of dark curls that would grow if she left it alone for long enough. Alex brushed his fingers through the strands, smiling when Margo's breath caught and her hips twitched up.

"And it was hot?"

"Ohhh yeah." Margo closed her eyes momentarily, recalling the scene. "The one needed a cock in him so badly he was practically crying."

Alex's smile widened. "Nice. Sounds like someone else I know when she's in a mood."

And with that, he lowered his head and brought his mouth to her pussy. He suckled gently at her outer labia before he parted them with the flat of his tongue and licked at her clit. It was a tiny thing, hidden entirely by its hood, so Margo needed lots of strong, concentrated attention to get it interested.

By the time it was, Margo was soaked to her thighs and even down to her ass with Alex's saliva. She clutched needily at his head while she rocked into his mouth, dragging her clit up and down the slick length of his tongue. Her back arched, and she panted and moaned.

She could have gone hours like that—and so could he, she knew from years of experience—but that wasn't what she wanted tonight. She wanted playful; she wanted something out of the ordinary.

"There were also," she said, with a waver in her voice, "tentacles involved. In the story. Not, mmm, not sure if I mentioned that."

Alex drew back—Margo had to remind herself to relax her grip—and blinked at her. His cheeks and chin were shiny with her wetness and smeared with a bit of white cervical mucous. One of his eyebrows lifted incredulously. "No there weren't."

Margo laughed. "No, there weren't. But there could've been. I'd have read it."

"Of course you would. Because you're a filthy girl." Alex laid a kiss to Margo's mons, firmly enough that she felt the sweet pressure against her clit. Then he raised himself to his hands and knees and crawled up her body. "Was that supposed to be some sort of hint?"

"Might've been." Margo slouched even lower, until only her head was still propped against the headboard, so that Alex could bring their mouths together. He smelled and tasted like her, which made her *ache*.

"You're ridiculous," he said after he pulled away, rolling his eyes although his tone was teasing.

"Yep." She wrapped her arms around his shoulders and beamed at him. "But you adore me."

The pronouncement made Alex's expression go soft. The lingering tension in his shoulders, which Margo hadn't even registered until now, melted away. "I do. I really do."

And with that, he climbed off the bed and walked to the closet, where they kept their toy box.

Originally, it had been something of a joke. An impulsive purchase made just past four in the morning, when during a bout of insomnia Margo had found the idea of owning a dildo shaped like a bluish-green octopus tentacle irresistibly hilarious. She definitely hadn't expected to like using it. The silicone was so soft it was almost squishy, which felt creepy in her hands, but in her *cunt*—oh, it was good. It moved with her, molded to her, didn't jab her if she or Alex slipped and found a bad angle. Not to mention, it was thick and curved and fit surprisingly well into their harness.

Margo loved it.

While Alex got the toy clean and ready, Margo shucked her

tank top and moved their lubricant within reach. Her arousal dimmed during the brief intermission, but flared again when she lay on her back cupping her vulva with one hand, sweeping her fingertips through the wetness gathered in her slit. She watched as Alex fastened the harness straps over his briefs, the tentacle dildo bobbing where it was attached.

When he was finished, he knelt on the bed between Margo's legs, which she spread wider to give him room.

"Is this how you want it?" he asked. He rested a hand on either of her inner thighs, stroking the skin there with his thumbs. "Should I make gurgling noises like an actual tentacle monster, or...?"

Margo laughed, which quickly became a moan when one of Alex's hands ventured higher and his fingers slid inside her and moved in a slow circle, opening her. "See if you can manage some ooze too," she said. Her voice had gone high and quivery. "If you don't mind."

Echoing her laugh, Alex removed his fingers and clambered forward on his knees until he could press the tip of the toy into her.

It burned—the good sort of burn, the kind that was so close to pleasure she could hardly tell the two apart. Her head fell back, her spine arched, and she hooked her legs around Alex's hips, drawing him close, which made the toy sink deeper. She could never get over how it felt to be penetrated. Like poking at a bruise, the stretch and the sensation of fullness were so strange yet also so immensely *satisfying*, although she couldn't pinpoint why no matter how she tried.

She basked in it, rolling her hips when Alex was completely in. He planted his hands on either side of her head and leaned over her, wearing a slack-jawed expression of awe that never failed to make her dizzy with satisfaction. Her pussy clenched around the toy, which sent an ache of pleasure through her so exquisite that she groaned, her eyes drifting shut.

"I'll see what I can do," Alex said.

By that point, Margo had forgotten what they were talking about, and she didn't particularly care. With her eyes still closed, she concentrated on the fullness, on how the toy's rounded, upturned tip dragged along the walls of her cunt and hit her sweet spot with every undulation of her hips. Alex stayed still, stroking the hair that had fallen out of her ponytail while he let her work herself on his cock.

"Good?" he murmured. "Is that what you needed? A good dirty fuck with my tentacle in your cunt?"

Margo's mouth went dry. "Yes." The word stuck in her throat. Opening her eyes, she licked her lips and tried again. "Yes. Just—let me get on my stomach."

She'd barely said it before Alex was pulling out and ducking out of the way so she could flip over and lie flat on her belly with her bottom up. This time, Alex paused to slick the toy from base to tip with lube before he guided it into her pussy.

The silicone was still warm, and with the lubricant, it glided smoothly in. But it felt thicker in this position—enough so that Margo's jaw dropped and she clutched at the pillow beneath her head, letting out a long, low moan as she was stretched. When Alex was seated, his hipbones pressing into her ass cheeks, she felt stuffed full, fit to burst. It was heavenly.

"All right?" Alex asked. He held Margo's waist, his thumbs tracing indiscriminate shapes in the small of her back. When she nodded, trying to find words, he bent forward until he was weighing her down and pinning her in place. "Good." His lips brushed her shoulder. "My gorgeous girl, taking my cock so well."

Margo shuddered, letting go of the pillow so she could put her hands between her thighs. She cupped her vulva, parting her labia and brushing her clit, which was hard now and peeking from its hood. When she thrust forward, it rubbed against her fingertips in a sweet, slick glide that made her toes curl and white-hot sparks dance across her vision.

Alex moved with her, thrusting in weak pulses that not only

moved his cock in and out of her, but also drove her harder into her own hand. In minutes, she was trembling and muffling her cries in the pillow.

She tried to stay quiet so she could hear Alex's murmured encouragement—things like "That's it" and "I don't even have to move, do I? Look at you, fucking yourself on me" and "Oh god, you're so hot"—but she couldn't. She was a whore for a thick cock in her, and with the pressure on her clit building and diminishing in a steady rhythm, the sensation was heightened, transformed. There was a continual throb of pleasure in her groin, her wet cunt clutching hungrily at Alex's cock, her clit swollen and needy.

She came with a throaty sob, humping again and again into her hand while her pussy fluttered, each clench sending waves of bliss through her so strong they made her thighs quiver.

In the aftermath, she lay gasping, moaning at every residual throb that went through her. Alex had frozen and remained that way until she'd quieted. Then he mashed his wet lips to her shoulder and asked, "Can you go again?"

Margo could, probably, but she didn't want to. Not now, anyway. She shook her head, reaching behind her to grope at Alex's hips and pull him closer, which succeeded in bringing his cock even deeper. So deep it made her whimper.

"You," she told him. "Come on."

It took a bit of coaxing to get him to stop worrying about her, but finally he gave in. He lifted his chest from her back, gripped her hips with both hands, and gave the first proper thrust. Not the weak, supplementary rocking he'd been doing, but a sharp forceful movement that plunged his cock into her cunt and then drew back until only the tip remained.

Margo embellished her cry slightly, wanting it mentally more than her body did physically, and soon Alex was *pounding* into her, hard enough that the bedroom filled with the sounds of his hips slapping her ass, the headboard banging against the wall, and Alex's grunts of exertion and deep gasping breaths.

It was almost too much. The friction, the constant push of silicone (squishy or not) back and forth over her G-spot and edging nearer and nearer to her cervix with every thrust, the barrage of sensation nearly overwhelming her already sensitive genitals. But it was *good*. Good like the drop down a roller coaster's steepest hill: half a second of "No, no" followed by a lingering, fervent "Oh god, yes, *again*."

It was powerful, exhilarating. She loved it.

"Fuck," Alex said. "Oh fuck." He pitched forward suddenly, letting go of Margo's hips so he could grip the sheets on either side of her shoulders instead. His pace turned frantic, and there was a waver in his voice as though he was close to tears. "God, I can—I can almost *feel* you. You're so, uh, so tight, hot—"

He was close, then. "Please," Margo said, more breath than voice. "Come in me. Please."

He did. Two more thrusts, and then he let out a loud "Ahh!" and fell forward, plastering his sweaty shoulders and damp binder to Margo's back and panting into her nape. His arms went around her, clinging while he recovered.

Tired and hot, brimming with a sudden surge of affection, Margo closed her eyes and relished his weight.

After several minutes spent catching his breath, Alex groaned as though he was just waking up. "God. Why don't we do that all the time? Food and bathroom breaks, and then just fucking you again and again the whole rest of the day."

But even as he said it, he was lifting off her. The tentacle toy caught briefly on the rim of Margo's cunt, and she grunted as it slipped free with a wet plop. "All the time? God. Maybe I *am* a bad influence on you."

"Of course you are," said Alex, flopping down beside her. His tone was lofty, teasing and fond. "The worst."

# LIGHTING THE PYRE

by Theda Hudson

Each pinprick is an irritant. The hum of the machine grates on my nerves not quite like nails on a chalkboard, but close. I will keep on, though, because this is my choice. I look down again. The tattoo artist is filling in the outline of the bird's head in brilliant red, green, blue, orange. Its outspread wings cover the three-inch scars that go across the center of my chest where my nipples would have been.

The privacy area is screened and just a little bigger than a curtained off hospital bed. It smells of sweat, ink and disinfectant. If I look at myself with the hand mirror, I can see my chest. My skin is just starting to get that old lady look with tiny wrinkles. Not bad for a forty-five-year-old woman, Darla always says.

The bird's head, rising up the center between where my breasts used to be, is gorgeous. I can see in his eye that he is confident, keen, proud—everything I used to be. Darla says I will be again. I wonder. Middle age is not what it's cracked up to be. I'm slower, stiffer and weaker than I want to be, than I should really be.

The space heater kicks on and the warmth is comforting on my bare flesh. I sip cold orange soda, smelling the crisp juice and tasting the bubbles as they sparkle in my mouth. It reminds me that I'm hungry. That's a good thing, a victory after a long, hard war.

I feel alive. The very idea is foreign, like running into an old friend you haven't seen since forever. You get a glimmer that makes you realize how beat down you've been, how exhausted, how depressed, how horrified.

It's over now. I can reclaim my life. Or, like Darla says, remake it. She's watching me from the other side of the tattooist. She is gorgeous for a fifty-year-old broad, just a little bit of a woman with curves that always have me running my hands over them. Her thick hair is dark and curly, and she goes limp like a kitten when I grab a handful at the nape of her neck and put her mouth where I want it.

She winks at me from behind her latest designer glasses—*eyewear*, she always corrects me—and sends me a smooch with full, red lips as she pinches a nipple on her plump boob through the tight V-neck tee. I wink back at her as I see that button rise up and press against the lacy low-cut bra. Yeah. So why don't I feel hopeful and confident? Why doesn't the heat burn between my legs, fill my chest and make my hands clench the way it used to? That's an old friend I'd really like to meet up with again.

Cancer takes away your choices. It's selfish, thoughtless and disdainful. It cares nothing for your hopes and dreams, churning them up in its relentless efforts to come out on top.

But I'm strong. I beat it the same way I have run over every obstacle in my life. I only had to run into it a lot to crush it, to push it down, out. Thank gawd for Darla. She was there every step of the way, cheering, soothing, caring. But I wonder if I've smashed myself flat, emptied myself against the constant battle to beat it.

The ink burns, or the needle does. I'm not sure which it is.

Pain shimmers over my skin. It's vibrant, the same way the ink is. Bright and sharp. That's something, too, and I own it, because it's mine, because I chose it.

"Okay," the tattooist says, sitting back and shutting the machine off. "Same drill," she says as she washes the bird's head with green soap, rinses it and covers it with a large bandage. "Keep it covered for a few hours. Use the A&D ointment for a day or so, and wash it with some neutral antibiotic soap to keep it clean. If you need lotion, use some plain Lubriderm. Call me if something doesn't feel right."

"Thanks, Carol. You're a doll," I say and give her a good smooch and a wad of cash.

Darla stands up. "That is so beautiful, Brin."

"Yeah, you were right. Cancer taketh away, and art giveth back." Ever since she found the tattoos for breast cancer survivors website, Darla pored over images, searching for the right one for me. She was with me every step of the way through the entire mess. We celebrated our third anniversary just after the surgery. When she showed me the picture of the bird in some book, the words were just sounds falling out of her mouth, the idea alien.

I want to believe she's right—and sometimes you have to fake it until you can make it. Now that it's nearly finished, I can sort of see her point, like a hole in the wall of a peep show.

"Come on," I say, slipping on my denim shirt and buttoning it up. "I'm hungry."

I think I can feel the ink settling into my skin. When I had the outline done, it felt like a shadow of me coming back out of a deep, dark hole. There's color now. I should be climbing out into the sunlight, bright and more than a shadow of my old self.

Mostly though, I'm angry. It's stupid because I never cared about my breasts. They were never part of my body image, more of an inconvenience. But cancer ravaged them until there were no options left but to dive in with a scalpel. I had no choice.

Darla opens the tattoo parlor door and whisks me out into

the waning light of early evening. The setting sun feels good on my face. Birds chirp as they swoop over the intersection up ahead, snapping up the bugs roiling in a cloud above the hot pavement.

She puts her arm through mine and presses her breast against my arm. I press back against that extravagant, soft pillow. A twinge flickers between my legs, spreading faint trails up into my belly. I press harder and she giggles, running her hand over my ass. I pull her in tighter, smelling sweat and the Poison perfume she put on this morning.

"Feel like walking over to Alfredo's?" she asks. "We can eat and then, if you're tired, I can walk back over and get the car."

"Sure. I could eat some linguini." I hate that she has to consider that I wouldn't have enough energy to get back to the car. But cancer does that to you. I started taking tai chi a week ago to build myself back up. It's good for concentration, for keeping those ugly thoughts at bay. And I can get through an entire class now without breaking into a sweat or teetering off balance.

She moves her arm around my waist and I lift mine to encircle hers, wincing a bit at the flicker of pain on the tattoo and the recovering muscles, but it's good, my choice, and I like it.

My mouth waters the moment we walk into the hole-in-the-wall restaurant with the wax-caked wine bottles sitting on tiny tables covered with red-and-white checked tablecloths.

We play footsie under the table, and she takes her shoe off and presses it between my thighs. Warmth wells up like she's blowing on embers and I rock my hips against her, feeling her foot mold around my strap-on. The warmth is a nice reminder of who I am. Smiling at each other, we sip wine, and Darla dings me not to eat all the bread and ruin my dinner.

Tony's cooking tonight. He knows us well and makes me a smaller plate. I have another half glass of wine while I slurp noodles and pick mussels out of their shells, dragging a thick heel of bread through the buttery drippings in the bottom of the bowl to capture the last drops.

Darla orders a piece of cake for dessert, but I only have a bite or two before I am completely full. My eyelids are heavy and I loll back in the chair, watching the moon rise through the big windows at the front. When the check comes, I pull my wallet out and Darla and I haggle, finally going dutch for the bill.

"You sit here and enjoy yourself," she says. "I'll get the car."

I'm so comfortable I don't even argue. But still, I feel like an old woman nodding over the dinner table. I want my life back. I want to move past this. I want the slumbering coals to wake up, and I want an evening with Darla that stokes them, if not to a roaring blaze, then a comfortable heat that will consume any lingering doubts and fears I have.

I see the lights of her Juke shine through the windows and I wave at Tony as I head for the door. My belly is full, the sting in my chest has subsided to a dull ache, and a beautiful woman is waiting for me to climb in the car with her.

As soon as I slam the door, her hand is on my crotch and her eyes are shiny in the twilight. I turn up the stereo and Euro industrial tech music blares out, the bass beating insistently against my body. I rock my hips forward and she runs a long, red nail up the front of my pants.

Reaching out, I tweak her nipple, laughing as she jerks. "Ow. That hurt."

"But look how hard it gets. And I know the pain shoots right down to your pussy." I move my hand down, turning it so I can clasp her crotch in my hand. Her pants are damp, hot like a jungle, and I lift my fingers to my nose, smelling her desire, then licking every finger. She is watching me intently, her mouth open, a bit of tooth showing in a way that I always find super hot.

"Hey, the road," I say, and she jerks her attention back to driving.

We are coming up on a turnoff that leads to a park. We've spent lots of time there, hiking, biking, lolling on the grass. "Turn in," I command. She looks at me for a long moment, then nods through a shit-eating grin.

The road is deserted, the parking lot nearly so. The moon is up and bright, silvering the trees that surround the lot on three sides. The trailhead is marked by a wooden fence and a red metal farm gate, which is still open. The wind soughs through leaves, and I hear an owl hoot somewhere off in the woods.

"You have the blanket in the back still?"

"I do. Do you have the energy?"

I lay a finger over her mouth, then trace her lips and push into her mouth. It's warm and wet, and she sucks and tongues it. The embers feel like someone blew over them, and I shiver suddenly as desire runs from the center of my chest where that proud bird's head sits, down into my crotch, pooling there.

"Forget the blanket. Let's walk," I tell her. We get out and she takes my hand as we head up the path. I can hear an owl hoot again and some rustling in the brush off the path. We walk up past the first curve that overlooks the city, speckled with lights like sequins on a quilt.

Darla pauses as we reach a large oak tree. "Yes," I say when she looks enquiringly at me. She makes her way under the branches, through a tangle of brush and around an elm tree. Then we're in the middle of a small copse of trees, a shaft of moonlight shining down like a spotlight, turning everything silver. I can smell leaves, rot and Darla as I stand, taking a deep breath, my hands on my hips.

I am alive. I am here in this moment with a beautiful woman who loves me, wants me.

Taking two strides, I push her against a tree and kiss her hard. She gives it back, pressing her tongue into my mouth and moaning against my teeth. She tastes of chocolate cake and wine, and the coals between my legs heat up, sending flickers of heat throughout my belly. I feel loose and liquid and welcome them like old friends to a party.

She tries to press her breasts against me, but I lean back. No pressure on the new ink. Instead, I pull her shirt up and the cups of her bra down. She loves the naughty wantonness of being exposed like this. It's not as exciting as doing it during the day where we might be seen by some random hiker, but still, it's outside.

My hands fit around her waist perfectly and she sighs in pleasure. A breeze makes her nipples harden, and I suck one, then the other, giving her a little tooth. Then I lick the mounds and bury my face between them, surrounded by her sweat and faint perfume.

"Ah," I growl, trying to urge the old friends to rev up and spread out, sending tingles of desire throughout my body.

I am alive. Tested, wounded, ravaged, but still kicking. I want to do this. But wanting isn't enough.

Biting her, I nibble my way around her breasts, leaving marks, as she squeals and squirms. Tomorrow she will spend time in front of the mirror admiring and showing them to me all day, smiling at me.

A breeze blows again, and she giggles as goose bumps rise up on her skin. When I kiss her, she groans and presses against my crotch, rolling her hips to some beat. She begins to hum and I know the song. My heart leaps as I remember the words.

*You are my life, I give myself to you, take me, have me, hold me, make me into what you want.*

Opening her pants, I pull them down. Darla loves this; it's naughty, which makes her embarrassed, which turns her on. Her quim is hot, moist, and her musky desire floats up between us. She rocks her hips, groaning when I slip my finger between them and skate over her clit. My own hips rock in time, and I can feel the heat rise like someone put a bellows to it.

Suddenly, I turn her to face the tree and push her against it.

Pulling her pants down, I smile as she shimmies her ass at me, and I playfully smack her smooth, white skin. Taking out my wallet, I retrieve a condom, tear it open with my teeth and shove the empty packet in my pocket. My pants are open in a flash and I slip it on. She moans as I grasp a knot of hair at the base of her neck and she goes completely pliable as she lifts her hips to meet mine.

The breeze caresses my ass and I feel a need to bare myself further. When I unbutton my shirt I pull off the bandage, shoving it in my pocket and exposing my chest to the world. The cool air is harsh on my tender flesh, and I wonder what the phoenix feels as it rises up off the ashes of its funeral pyre.

Is it angry that it had to start over, regretful about lost opportunities, depressed about the end of its former life?

I realize it doesn't matter. It's new, it's fresh, cleansed by the purifying flame. The phoenix chose to build its pyre, chose to climb on, chose to light it and be reborn.

Just like I chose to fight, chose to try every treatment, and finally, chose to go under the knife. I've come through the trial cured. I'm alive and a beautiful woman is waiting for me to have her, claim her, bring her—and me—to a glorious incandescence of our own.

Darla lifts her hips and arches her back as I drive into her. The heat from her pussy on my hips radiates like burning embers as I thrust into her. Her musk fills my nose. An answering wave of heat in my own sex burns with pleasure. Every scorching stroke reminds me that I survived, that I won no matter the cost, and together Darla and I work to create a blaze that explodes nearly simultaneously for us.

My orgasm pushes a cry from me that I imagine echoes the phoenix's on my chest, shrieking as it lifts off from its funeral pyre, brilliant wings beating against the last embers of the fire that birthed it.

Darla moans, a deep cry wrung from her soul, and lets her

head fall, exhausted.

I rest my arms on her shoulders as we heave deep breaths in the wake of the inferno we created. After long moments, I pull out, and when Darla stands, I take her in my arms.

It seems I have found my own pyre.

"Now that is one way to light a fire," I say.

"I'll say," she whispers, her breath hot against my neck.

Now all that remains is for me to take flight with my new life. That's my choice.

# RESTITUTION

by Ria Restrepo

I knew they were watching me. In the corner of the interrogation room, a camera was mounted near the drop ceiling. As the red light blinked, I wondered how many were monitoring the live feed. Then there was the two-way mirror right across from me. Was the observation room behind it filled to capacity?

My senses were hyperaware; everything was sharp and bright. The silence rang in my ears, and beyond my own light perfume, a mustiness lingered from the sweat of all the people who'd been where I was at that moment. My nerves were alive with fear—and, if I was honest, more than a little excitement too. It was similar to the feeling I got right before a show.

The headlines and sound bites flashed in my head: *Ella Lopez Arrested for Shoplifting! Good Girl Goes Bad! Pop Star in the Slammer! Klepto Cubana Cutie! Little Havana Hottie in Hand-cuffs!*

My first album launched me into stardom, but my second was a major disappointment by comparison. There was a lot of talk about me being a one-hit wonder. My third album would drop soon, and I needed another hit at the top of the charts or my short career would be over. How I handled this situation could make all the difference.

Shifting on the hard chair made my short skirt ride up even higher on my thighs. If my legs fell open even a little, I'd flash my skimpy panties. Carefully crossing one leg over the other, I tried to tug my skirt down as much as possible. It was difficult with one hand cuffed to the metal table in front of me.

I licked my glossy lips, wishing I had something to drink. They were trying to make me squirm and it was working. The anticipation built every moment I sat there...imagining what would happen next.

Finally, the door opened. Officer Hernandez stood in the doorway for a moment, just looking at me, his expression giving nothing away. Then he entered and closed the door behind him with a firm, ominous *snick*. My heart rate picked up and I shifted in my seat again.

He was really quite impressive, his tall, well-muscled body barely contained by his crisp uniform. His military buzz cut, strong jaw and dark-brown eyes gave him a steely, no-nonsense appearance. His confident bearing commanded my respect, and I sat up a little straighter.

The man did something to me I hadn't experienced with anyone else. When he first put me in handcuffs, my heart raced, and I felt surprisingly achy between my legs. Even now, my panties were getting very damp. And I irrationally craved his approval.

My pulse thrummed in my ears as he walked to the table and placed a bottle of water in front of me, his gaze locked onto mine.

"Thank you." I quickly opened the bottle and took a few much-welcome sips.

His gaze dropped to my mouth, wandered down my throat to my very prominent cleavage where it lingered for a moment, and then moved on, landing on my crossed legs. I briefly wondered if uncrossing them and exposing myself would help my cause.

"You're in a great deal of trouble, Ms. Lopez," he said, his eyes once again on mine.

I placed the bottle back on the table. "This has all been a terrible mistake. I swear, I wasn't stealing."

"So you accidentally walked out of a store wearing earrings worth more than most people make in a year?"

"Well...yes."

Officer Hernandez crossed his arms over his broad chest, his bulging biceps straining the material of his shirt. "No one's going to believe that, you know? You're just another spoiled little celebrity who thinks she can get away with anything."

"Honestly, I tried on the earrings, and then the salesperson was showing me other things and I forgot I even had them on."

He arched one eyebrow. "You forgot you had on earrings worth a hundred grand?"

This time I did uncross my legs and leaned forward a bit for good measure. With my plunging halter top and my skirt hem practically at my hips, I was clearly displaying my lace-covered pussy and tits.

"Listen, officer, is there anything I can do to make this all go away? I'll pay anything."

Bracing his arms on the table, he leaned toward me. "Are you offering to bribe a police officer?"

"No!" I pulled back and quickly explained, "I meant I'd pay for the earrings. It'll be just like I bought them. I'll even pay more than the jeweler wanted...for his inconvenience. You know, what's it called? Oh, *restitution*!"

His eyes bored into mine. "You'll pay for them?"

"Sure," I said with a shrug, "it's not a problem."

Static crackled through a speaker in the wall before a deep voice over the intercom said, "The shop owner said she can pay for the earrings."

Releasing a deep breath, I slumped back in my seat.

"But he wants something else before he'll drop the charges," the voice continued.

I jerked upright in the chair. "I'll do whatever he wants."

"Anything?"

"Anything!"

"For her to learn her lesson, he thinks she needs a spanking."

I gasped. "A spanking?"

"Twenty hard smacks on her bare ass from Officer Hernandez."

Standing with his hands fisted on his hips, Officer Hernandez's eyes gleamed with wicked delight. "So what's it going to be, princess?"

I forced a swallow through my suddenly tight throat. It was unorthodox, but I needed to take the punishment to save my career. "Okay, I'll do it."

He pulled a key out of his pocket and unfastened me from the handcuffs. "Bend over the table and lift your skirt over your pretty ass."

Slowly, I stood on rubbery legs, pushing my chair back. When I started to bend forward, he stopped me.

"No, over here," he said, motioning to the other side of the table.

He wanted my ass facing the two-way mirror, so they'd see everything. Taking a deep breath, I walked around the table and faced away from the mirror. Pulling my stretchy skirt up over my backside—not that it had far to go—I leaned forward and rested my forearms on the cold tabletop.

My heart pounded in my chest; my breathing was fast and shallow. My long black hair fell down into my face, almost cocooning me. But even so, my cheeks burned with humiliation, because I knew my G-string left my ass completely exposed and vulnerable.

"Mmm, very nice," Officer Hernandez said from just behind me.

I felt him move closer until his hip touched mine. He brushed the hair away from one side of my face and pushed it over my shoulder. Then he leaned over me, so his lips teased my ear. "I'm not going to take it easy on you."

All I could do was nod. I knew this was going to hurt, but that just made me wetter.

"I want you to sing for me, little diva. Call out the numbers."

"Yes, sir," I said, my voice raspy and unfamiliar.

He shifted away from me and I held my breath, awaiting the first blow. When it came, it was hard, punishing, brutal—everything I thought it would be. My body lurched forward, jostling the table enough to knock the water bottle onto the floor.

"One," I cried out on a pent-up gust of air.

Then came the next smack on the opposite cheek, and I called that one out too. There was a mean sting on my skin when his large hand first made contact, followed by a deep ache in my flesh as it absorbed the full force of the strike. He spread the slaps around, alternating sides, occasionally landing near the juncture between my thighs—those were the best ones.

Each time, the pain roared throughout my body, making my nipples throb and my cunt clench in sympathy. But it was a delicious torture that built with the burn until I was on fire. I could feel my juices sliding past my cunt lips and onto my thighs. I couldn't believe it; I was going to come, just from him spanking me.

I sang my restitution until I almost wailed toward the end. "Twenty" came out as a strangled whimper as a violent orgasm tore through me. I collapsed onto the table, unable to hold myself up any longer. Pressing the side of my face against the cool metal surface, I tried to get control of my breathing. I realized my cheeks were wet with tears.

"That'll do," the intercom voice declared. "The charges are dropped."

Getting myself together, I pushed up from the table and carefully stood on shaky legs. I pulled my skirt down over my very sore ass. Sitting was going to be a problem for a while.

Turning around, I found Officer Hernandez leaning against the mirror, his eyes intense and magnetic. "So, he's satisfied." His lips curved up into a devastating smile. "And you've been satisfied. But what about me?"

"You?" I asked, wiping the tears from my eyes.

"Yes. I lose a high-profile bust and I'm left with a major hard-on for my trouble."

"Oh," I said, taking in the massive bulge in his slacks. I worried my bottom lip for a moment, then gave him the coy smile I was famous for. "I guess I should make restitution to you as well."

My brown eyes locked onto his. I walked to him and knelt at his feet as gracefully as possible. Watching his face to make sure I wasn't going too far, I brushed my tear-stained cheek against his crotch, nuzzling his erection through his pants.

Groaning, he threaded his fingers through my hair and gently held the back of my head.

Encouraged, I reached up and began unfastening his trousers. Once I had him unbuttoned and unzipped, his slacks fell down his muscular legs. The boxer briefs he wore underneath left little to the imagination. I pressed my nose into the soft, warm cotton between his rigid cock and heavy balls, and breathed in his musky, masculine scent.

"Fuck," he said, his grip on my hair tightening.

Looking up, I saw his eyelids drooping a bit and his mouth slightly open. I kissed the base of his cock through the material, then slowly pulled down the waistband, freeing him. I couldn't completely get my hand around his proud length, he was so big. The head was already wet, so I licked it, tasting his salty essence. Then I wrapped my lips around the knob and sucked lightly.

"Oh yeah, that's it," he said with a moan.

I loved that I was affecting him that way, and he felt so good in my mouth. My cunt was throbbing again, begging me to rub it and relieve the pressure, but I knew I needed to focus on him.

Taking more of him in my mouth, I cupped his balls with one hand while I stroked the base of his cock with the other.

"God yes, take it in your hot little mouth."

Fondling his balls, I took him deeper and deeper until he was nudging my throat. My gaze never leaving his, I began sucking up and down his shaft, my tongue caressing the underside and then swirling around the tip when I got to the head.

"Damn, you have a wicked tongue."

His chest heaved and he lightly pulled my head forward, urging me to go even farther.

Moaning, I sucked him harder and faster, jerking the base of his cock with my hand in synchronized strokes. My other hand softly squeezed his balls as I took him as deep as I could and swallowed, massaging the head of his prick.

"Christ, Ella...I'm going...to come."

Increasing the pressure on his dick even more, I sped up my hand and worked my mouth along his length even faster. I was so turned on I had to press my thighs together to relieve some of the ache in my pussy.

With a loud roar, he came in my mouth in powerful, thick bursts. Humming at his rich, tangy flavor, I swallowed it all down as fast as I could, but there was so much a little seeped out onto my lips. I kept sucking him, savoring him, until I'd milked every last drop.

As I let his softening cock slide out of my mouth, I watched his breathing even out and his eyes become more focused. Taking his hand from my hair, he dragged his thumb over my bottom lip and captured the runaway stream of come. I took his thumb into my mouth and licked it clean.

"Good girl," he said and gave me a lazy smile.

I was radiant with his approval.

He helped me to my feet and then quickly pulled up his underwear and pants.

"Well, you're free to go now, Ms. Lopez," he said as he fastened and zipped his slacks. "Just stay out of trouble, okay?"

"Yes, sir."

After opening the door, he guided me out of the interrogation room with his palm on my back.

"Thank you, Ray," I said, using his first name once we were in the hallway. "I really owe you for this."

Smiling down at me, he pulled me against his body. "And I plan to collect, little girl."

We'd known each other for a while, and I was hopelessly addicted to his dominant nature. He made me light up in a way no one else ever had, and I trusted him implicitly.

"What about the shop owner?" I asked.

"Oh, he was very understanding and didn't want to press charges." His smile turned feral. "I convinced him that you should at least be brought in for a stern talking to. So you'd learn your lesson."

"Mmm, yes, I most certainly did."

Just then, the door to the observation room opened and Ray's best bud, Derek, walked out, grinning like an idiot. He handed Ray what I assumed was the recording of the incident in the interrogation room.

"Thanks, man," Ray said. "I'll catch up with you in a few minutes."

"Sure thing." Derek gave him a slap on the shoulder and then winked at me. "That was some performance, Ella."

I could feel my face burning as he walked away.

"Was he the only one in there watching?" I asked Ray.

"Of course," he said, grasping my chin between his thumb and index finger. "I wouldn't let anyone else watch my girl get her sweet little *culo* spanked."

I laughed. "Well, soon everyone's going to see it."

"Not live and in person."

"True. So, you'll make sure the recording gets leaked?"

"Yes, but you better come through with those private security jobs," he said, lightly squeezing my tender ass, "because this stunt'll definitely cost us our jobs."

"I promise, you'll both be my personal bodyguards." I leaned into him, pressing my breasts against his chest. "But only you will own me completely."

A growl rumbled up from deep in his chest, and he gave me a brief, hard kiss. "Go home and keep your eyes on the news."

"Yes, sir."

As I left the police station and stepped into the Miami sunshine, I couldn't help smiling. By the following week, my new single, "Punish Me," would be a number-one hit, because this kind of scandal was always good for sales.

# THE CARNALARIUM

by Rose Caraway

"Oh, awesome!" It was the GoPro camera and GPS package I considered getting when I was restocking my travel supplies. "And an extra battery? You shouldn't have, Kendra!" I leaned forward, hooked a finger under her chin, then kissed her glossy, smiling lips. Kendra vibrated with pride at having earned such praise. But then there came that all too familiar push-peck sensation. It always started at the back of my neck—gently nudging at first, coaxing. If I put it off for too long, it became more insistent, impatient, a sharp pecking at my spine—a mother bird forcing her too-big offspring to get the fuck out of her nest already. I pulled away a little too quickly and Kendra's happiness faltered.

And there it was, that look. Accusatory hate, self-doubt and (the big one) *hope*, all sparkling in her beautiful, light-blue eyes. But this was par for the course. Although with Kendra, my leaving was a little different. I couldn't escape the other nagging sensation, deep in my chest. A thudding, heavy achiness. I thought I might love her.

Kendra looked up at me from her knees, tried to pretend

that her sorrow wasn't sucking the air out of the room. She sat between my legs, me on the couch, her on the floor. Reminding me of what an insensitive ass I could be sometimes. "I already put your account together, so no excuses. You better tweet every day, Beth, just so that I know where you are—that you're not dead." She let her fingers slide up my bare thighs, wooing me with her delicate touch. Goosebumps erupted over my flesh. My nipples hardened, guilt temporarily shoved back by the sweet little jolt of arousal that swirled in my belly.

"Just for you." I purred against her pouty lips. I slipped my tongue inside her mouth, pulled her short frame closer, tried to be who I was before *the restlessness* had taken hold of me. But, even as I said the words I knew she hoped to hear, I was lying.

I pulled her baby-pink camisole off, admired the way her long bronze locks zinged and zapped their staticky, messy protest. Then my eyes settled on her breasts. Much fuller than my own and pierced with shiny silver barbells—a gift from me on our third date, they were truly magnificent. Kendra was a full-figured, adorable girl with a body anyone could get lost in. Ignoring emotion, I chose impulse and reached for those breasts, hardened the pale little nipples between my fingers and thumbs, twisting the silver barbell piercings, memorizing their silkiness for the lonely nights ahead. The GoPro travel kit was forgotten amidst the wrapping paper. I kissed Kendra, desperate for her to know that I wanted to say thank you for the time we'd shared, and goodbye—because I *was* going to miss her. I read somewhere that a single kiss could accomplish such a task, but I couldn't seem to make it work.

Kendra did her best to seduce me, keep me here, but I simply couldn't stay. Being tied down to anything, including lovers, brought the walls closing in on me, threatening to block out the sunlight I craved. Kendra and I had been lovers for the better part of a year, but *the restlessness* had my heels itching to break for freedom, and the next two weeks were going to be difficult. I'd never been able to lay down roots, anywhere—with anyone—for any extended period of time. I'm what you might call a free spirit. I only rent month-to-month, own a throw-away cell phone, and I never stay with a partner for longer than a few fun-filled months before I flit away to explore some other part of the world, literally. I guess I might be afraid that if I stay put for too long, I might miss something else more fulfilling. To date, Kendra was my longest commitment. I took a certain amount of pride in that fact, but I couldn't ignore the wearying effect it was having on me. I'm just not...monogamous. With anything.

Kendra, my sweet, darling Kendra, is truly a girl who would be lost without someone to take care of her. I know that sounds borderline misogynistic, but it's true. She needs to be cherished like doll that she is. I can't leave her broken. Hurt is one thing, but *broken*? That guilt would eat at me for a long time.

I'm the complete opposite. I need to get out, away—experience life, people, the world. I've done everything from skydiving in New Zealand and Dubai to swimming through the labyrinth of lava tubes around Hawaii. I've already backpacked across Europe a few times, helped build homes for humanity in Mexico, hiked the Incan Trail, even followed a camera crew to Namibia and photographed two separate nomadic tribes in the jungles of Africa. Now it was time to traverse my own country. The good ol' USA—from the West Coast to the East Coast—*on foot*. With only two weeks left and still so much to do, my shopping list was getting longer and longer. At the top of that list—batteries. I simply couldn't forget batteries, or I'd be up shit creek without an orgasm. Screw the water purifying tablets. I needed my big O's more than water.

"I got you something else," Kendra breathed against the nape of my neck, bringing me out of my mental list of to-dos. The warmth caused me to be a lot more than a little juicy between the legs. I didn't want any more presents; I wanted Kendra to make me come.

"You did?" My voice was the best sultry-sweet I could manage.

"Yep." Kendra was trying so hard to be strong for me.

"What is it?" I asked.

She pulled a nondescript red envelope from beneath the couch. "I got us into The Carnalarium."

"The what?"

"*The Carnalarium.*" She rolled her eyes, a cute bratty expression I'd developed a liking for. I resisted grabbing her hair and throwing her over the couch cushions for a thorough spanking that was sure to lead to an extended fucking. "It's only the most popular sex dungeon in the city. I emailed the head Mistress a couple of months ago," she finally responded. "She said my application was interesting. She actually met me for coffee. We talked about a bunch of stuff—"

"You had coffee together?" I accused. I instantly regretted my tone. I was more surprised than anything; Kendra never went anywhere on her own.

"Nothing happened."

"I'm sorry, I'm just surprised is all. And kind of impressed." I was relieved to see the tension ease from her body.

"Really?" she asked, eyes lighting back up. Damage repaired.

"I remember the place. That old renovated abbey over on Rosary Hills, right?"

"Yeah. You wanna come with me?" This time that shy, blushing demeanor was too much to resist.

"Girl, I always want to come with you." I pulled her in, my kisses demanding. I slipped a hand between her legs and decided I'd let her come first.

The Carnalarium was a restored Abbey that, fortunately for the kink culture, didn't qualify as a historical landmark. Private money put it back together, and it was better for it. It was a rotunda architecture that had four adjoining apses converted into waiting rooms. The decor throughout was predictable antique Victorian furniture, but without all the gaudy lace trappings. There were several small and medium-sized erotic oil replicas hanging on the walls. A restored brushed-velvet settee, a fainting couch and an ornately designed mahogany armoire to stow personal belongings in. Everything felt lush, welcoming. We'd already gone over the rules and regulations, signed our contracts and provided proper blood work documentation, which nearly took two weeks. I'd been worried that our last playdate wouldn't happen.

We'd stripped down nearly twenty minutes ago, the wait making our nerves a little giddy. Playful kisses and pinches kept us occupied. Dee, the Mistress, would be there any moment to personally escort us to the main floor. Neither of us had been with a man in over a year, but Kendra said that the Mistress had found a great match.

"So...you're really up for this? Balls? Cock? Hairy chest?" I asked. It had been long enough for me that merely mentioning those body parts made *Mamma want.*

"Yes, but only if you still want to." Kendra's meek voice cracked. I didn't like how it made me immediately reach for her. I pushed her against the red-and-black baroque damask-printed wall. I knelt down, eased Kendra's thighs apart, then slipped my tongue deep into her slit. Kendra was a staunch believer in regular waxing, and I always appreciated how easily my tongue glided over such smooth, slippery little pussy lips.

I stiffened my tongue, pushed in deeper—reached it so far back that I could tickle the tight rim of her anus. My nose was smashed against her pubic bone as I flicked. The scent of pussy made me growl and salivate. Kendra tilted her pelvis, offering me a little more depth. I obliged. Then I dipped into her pussy hole. In and out, tasting. I moaned as low as I could, the vibrations fluttering up into Kendra's belly the way she always liked. Her pretty moans filled the waiting room, making my pussy swell and moisten in response. I scooted closer, my knees cushioned by lush carpet, and gripped Kendra's ample thighs. I moved my tongue a little farther up, teased and coaxed her sensitive clitoris from its fleshy shelter. The little nub responded almost immediately. I moaned and inserted three fingers pads up, and fucked her. Kendra came in seconds.

The heavy carved door whispered open. It was Dee, the Mistress of The Carnalarium.

From my knees I glanced up at Kendra, wiping my come-covered lips with the back of my hand. A shiny pink flush spread across her cheeks, indicating that she wasn't quite ready to vocalize even a simple greeting.

"Hi, sorry, we got a little carried away."

"The Captain is waiting for you." Mistress Dee arched a single painted-black eyebrow, then pushed the thick wooden door the rest of the way open. She signaled us to follow with a half-smile.

Arm in arm, we followed The Mistress down a refurbished red-brick hallway that echoed her boot heels, and introduced our ears and skin to the vibrations of a cacophony of voices caught in the throes of passion. The main room was an open, circular floor plan with what looked to be about twenty different stations lining it all the way around. From each station, men and women were reveling in various positions and stages of fucking. Kendra and I gasped in unison, our breaths taken away momentarily by the opulence surrounding us. From any angle anyone could observe the uncensored debauchery around them. Center to the newly glossed concrete floor, and below an enormous, polished brass chandelier of sconced cupids, was a leather sitting area where patrons could satisfy their voyeuristic leanings, 360 degrees around.

"What do the lights mean?" I inquired. The canned lighting put a kind of swanky, modern edge to the place that kind of worked, but kind of didn't.

Mistress Dee responded with only the slightest rehearsed tone. "Red signifies that the individual is occupied, or waiting for an appointment to show. Green represents that they are available for walk-ins. Yellow means occupied, but open for walk-ins, at their discretion."

"Oh." That was simple enough.

The Mistress pointed one painted-red nail toward a very tall, very naked man standing on the opposite side of the round room, his red light boldly glowing above his station. Kendra's nerves kicked in again and she glommed on to my arm, her bountiful breasts compressed nicely. The man stood, his feet shoulder width apart, his cock hanging, slightly swollen—presumably from his own anticipation. In his hands, he held a small molded-leather box about the size of a small shoebox.

I felt Kendra's arms loosen; her cheeks suddenly took on a strange pinkness. Something unsettling crept up my spine. I glanced back at *The Captain*. He was staring pointedly at Kendra. Jealousy triggered my jaw to clench. Mistress Dee's voice made me jump. "Your applications didn't mention any toys, devices or themed costumes, but if you change your mind, please push the com button and I will send an attendant over." My gaze was captured by a scantily clad maid walking by with a bucket of water in one hand and a sponge and yellow rubber gloves in her other. She was headed for a man chained to a St. Andrew's cross, stationed on our immediate left. Three other men, with exhausted but satisfied expressions on their faces, were just leaving.

Kendra's gaze, however, was still held by The Captain. "Oh, Captain. My Captain." She breathed those words so softly, I doubted she even knew she'd spoken them aloud. I couldn't say why, but I didn't like the sound of those words.

The Captain nodded politely then motioned to Kendra with one long finger. I felt her shiver under his inflexible command. She swallowed, her body trembling as she drifted away from me—ignoring me altogether for the first time in our relationship. My sweet, devoted Kendra seemed spellbound. Her small, bare feet carried her away, leaving my chest feeling strangely hollow. I reached out for her, but I was too late. She was already gone.

The Captain slid his long, tanned fingers through her rich cinnamon-colored hair like possessive talons, until they settled behind her neck, a gesture that had me clenching my jaw again. I resisted the knee-jerk instinct to embarrassingly shout, *She's mine!* When Kendra closed her eyes and raised her soft lips to meet his, my bones felt cold. They kissed for too long, and then this towering, naked stranger, holding the leather box, leaned down and whispered something into Kendra's ear. She turned, looked back at me, her eyes glossy, her cheeks pink with a lust that I hadn't seen in a long while. Her beautiful breasts rose and fell with slow, deep breaths, the silver piercings glinting with the captured red from The Captain's overhead light. I stepped forward, impulse once again reigning over emotion. But The Captain held up a hand, stopping me before I got too close. I'd never been halted by anything in my life.

"Kendra tells me that you are leaving her," he said, his deep tone on the edge of accusatory.

My mouth felt dry. "Yes, but..."

"To go 'see the world.'" He made it sound so *callous*.

"Well, yes...but..."

"Take this." He held up an ornamental globe, a miniaturized version of the planet Earth. "Hold it out, like so." Unthinking, I did as he said, an unusual thing for me. Then, over the echoes of our neighbors, I heard the distinct peel-and-rip sound of duct tape. Kendra pulled a strip from a roll. Before pasting it over my mouth, I saw something in her eyes that I had never seen before. *Autonomy.*

"As you won't be able to speak, your 'signal' will be to drop this. If the glass breaks, everything stops." I stood dumbly, my mind racing. What was happening? I *hated* the way Kendra kept smiling up at him so earnestly.

"Ready, kitten?" The Captain motioned to a simple chair I hadn't noticed before. Kendra guided me backward until the backs of my thighs touched the wooden edge, and then she pressed my shoulder until I sat down, her newfound confidence giving her a strength I found quite mesmerizing.

"*These* are for you, kitten." From the small leather box, The Captain pulled out a set of long gold chains attached to nipple clamps. *That must have been where the duct tape and glass globe came from.* At each opposite end, gold sailor's anchors swayed heavily. Kendra lifted her chin, thrust her breasts outward. Nonchalantly, The Captain unscrewed and then removed each of the silver barbells I'd gifted her. As he then threaded the new piercings through her nipples it hit me, in a ton-of-bricks sort of way. He was claiming her as his—and she wanted him to. The weight of the chains and clamps pulled Kendra's pale nipples downward, her expression reflecting that nothing else existed in her mind just then but that tugging sensation. *Off with the old and on with the new.*

"Don't move." The Captain then dragged an exceptionally tall black leather ottoman and placed it directly in front of my chair. I was forced to spread my legs so that the two pieces of furniture almost butted up against one another. I sat there, my shoulder aching from extending my arm out this long, trying to not crush the glass globe in my straining hand. The voices of impassioned people echoed around us, spanking, moaning, screaming, begging—all of it making me break out into a sweat. My pussy ached when Kendra propped herself over the ottoman. She adjusted a little, making sure to drape the gold chains prettily in front of her presented breasts. She held each clamp up and waited.

The Captain adjusted Kendra's hips, making sure her feet were spread adequately. Then he came around and took the gold clamps from her and clipped them, one at a time, to my nipples as though he'd done this to me every day. I groaned behind the duct tape; as he applied each one, my muffled breaths filled my cheeks with too much air. I blinked. The pain, exquisite. I panted through my nose. Kendra moaned next, open mouthed, as The Captain placed one hand on his cock and one on the ottoman. While stroking himself he gave the glider a slow, steady nudge. The gold chains became taut between us, extending mine and Kendra's nipples simultaneously. I moaned low in my throat, allowing the sharp tension to wash over me. The Captain let the tension rest, then he pushed the ottoman again. I shut my eyes, had to lean forward, give the chain slack. The glass globe—my world—almost slipped past my slackened grip.

"Beth." It was The Captain, his warning voice pulling me back into the moment. "Sit back. Keep your eyes open." He pushed again. Kendra's heavy breasts lifted at each tug of the piercings. The Captain repeated this multiple times, stroking to Kendra's cries. Then he halted the glider. Kendra turned toward his offered cockhead. Her little pink tongue reached for a taste. I was all but forgotten. My fingers trembled as I recovered, but the globe didn't fall.

Kendra pulled his tip into her mouth. She suckled and I groaned, hoping she'd take him deeper. The Captain withdrew himself and looked at me. I shied away, couldn't bear the disarming intensity. But he put a finger beneath my sweaty chin and forced me to look up. I'd never looked *into* someone so deeply before.

"Are you ready?"

In the back of my mind, I knew what he was really asking. The moment he'd beckoned Kendra to him, I knew what I had to do. I needed to let *her* leave *me*. Kendra deserved that much. I nodded. Tears threatened to fall. I didn't want her to leave me. It hurt too much. The Captain smiled. He unclipped the clamps, one nipple at a time. The duct tape pulled when I grimaced at the blood forcing nerve endings back to life. He clipped the gold clamps together into makeshift reigns. The Captain's face changed then; his eyes became brighter. He resumed his position behind Kendra, never letting go of her golden reigns.

I watched one and then two long, glistening strands of precome stream from his swollen tip as he rounded on Kendra. He whispered so sweetly to her, petted her flesh as he lowered his hips and took aim. Kendra reached for my thighs. I tucked my right hand under my thigh, while holding my left out. With one thrust, The Captain took possession of her, and the ottoman launched forward. Kendra grunted. My fingers trembled, but held that globe securely. The Captain thrust again and Kendra's breasts were tugged by her new reigns, the golden anchors sparkling gloriously. Her breath was ragged while I silently kept out my arm. Sweating. Letting her go. They moved in concert, bound by those two anchors.

I realized now that I'd selfishly left Kendra with no options... no choices but emptiness and disconnectedness. Now, we were parting on mutual terms. The Captain filled her, anchored her. Kendra's fingers became claws, digging into my thighs, her breasts heaving forward even as they were tugged back. Her mouth opened; she came loudly, freely, grounded in a way that I never could have provided.

I sobbed behind the duct tape, my globe still in one piece. My heart splintered.

# WAITING TO PEE

## by Amy Butcher

I watch with interest as an ant leans its front quarters out from the blade of grass, tasting at my bare toe with its antennae. I can almost hear the twitch, the rub of funiculi to skin.

"Tasty?" the ant brain ponders.

"Yes," it decides, and commits to a stretch across the abyss.

Cynthia babbles on beside me. It's more about her cleaners or her workout or something equally inane. I hardly listen, and she hardly notices. To the world, we are a beautiful couple—my butch to her femme creating a tender balance. To us, things are not that clear. There was a time when she was an ant and I was her picnic. Her fascination with me was resolute. But now, since we pledged monogamy, she has definitely changed insect species. Her ant has transmuted into one of those annoying deer flies, buzzing back and forth before my line of sight. No matter how much I try to brush her away, she just keeps coming back.

"I'm gonna go pee," I say, pulling on my sneakers.

I know she hears me because her story line changes. Without missing a beat, she's telling me about her last Dyke March at

Dolores Park and how she waited forever in the Porta-Potty line only to have one of the Sisters of Perpetual Indulgence get her habit's wimple stuck in the doorway. I definitely stop listening at this point.

"Be right back," I say as I stand and start sliding down the grassy hill.

It's not a Dyke March day, just another foggy Thursday afternoon, so I get to go to the real bathroom. The line is short: a Bettie Page femme already peeking in the door to see her reflection in the mirror, a hippy girl taking a break from her hula-hooping, two suburban teens who are already drunker than they should be at this time of day giggling with each other and a trans man last in line.

The trans man looks like he meant to pull into a truck stop, not this hipster haven. His U-Haul baseball cap is tipped back and to the side. His white tank is frayed under the arms, the edge of his chest binder visible above the curve of material stained yellow with sweat.

"Hey," he says as I step into the back of the line.

"Hey," I nod, playing my part in the ritual of masculine-identified greeting. As a butch, I've come to know this acknowledgement as one of mutual respect. It is the gesture of cowboys tipping their hat with one hand while fingering the handles of their holstered six-shooter with the other. Acknowledgement, assessment and admonition all rolled up into one single word.

"The men's room here is disgusting," he says by way of explanation before turning back towards the front of the line.

It takes me a moment to understand why my heart has just clenched in my chest, why my spine has hunched imperceptibly as if taking a blow. He's trying to tell me why he stands here in *this* line for the women's room and not on the other side of the building for the men's. He's trying to justify this no-win choice he's made, one he has had to make hundreds of times before. He's telling me of his shame.

"I hear you," I say to his back, really wanting to wrap this trucker into my arms.

Bettie Page is in and out of a stall in a flash and is now spreading out her make-up before the graffiti-scratched mirrors.

Hippy Girl is distracted. She flips her dreadlocked hair back and forth, rattling the beads on the ends against her uplifted palms as she counter-swivels her hips. Her eyes are closed as she tries to find the syncopation to some music playing only in her imagination.

"Ah, excuse me," the teenager ventures. Her friend giggles beside her.

No response.

"I think there's an empty," she says, tapping Hippy Girl on the shoulder and pointing. Hippy Girl smiles and nods then disappears into one of the three stalls, wrestling her glittery hoops in beside her.

Our line moves up one more position.

I scan the crowd and wonder if Cynthia is still talking out loud or if, lacking an audience, she has actually quieted. She has told me that having a sounding board really helps her work things out. But she never wants me to respond. She says it interrupts her thinking. This leaves me feeling like the very board she wants me to be—rigid and inanimate. I know I need to shift this pattern but sometimes the options are few, getting up to pee often the path of least resistance. I've no doubt Cynthia has pulled out her phone, finding someone else to pick up with right where she left off with me.

The bathroom line has hardly moved and I don't care.

A rattle of hula-hoops as Hippy Girl emerges from the far stall. She pauses by the sinks for just a moment. Bettie Page is still hard at work occupying the breadth of the space. Hippy Girl just shrugs and steps outside. "Sunshine cleans everything!" she exclaims, lifting her face towards the foggy sky. "Hmm?" she says, shrugs again, and heads off towards her tribe of spinners.

The near stall opens. A pencil-thin hipster emerges. She's been in there forever. She wrestles to pull up her tight jeans even as gravity pulls her thick-framed glasses down. One corner of her plaid shirt has caught awkwardly in her zipper and it takes her a moment to wrest it free.

Before anyone else can move, Bettie Page scoops up her belongings and shoots into the stall. Again.

One of the suburban girls has started to sway. Her friend tucks an arm around her waist, growing steadier on her feet as her friend grows even wobblier. "We're almost there. *Do not* puke on me, whatever you do." Scolding and supporting, she guides her friend into the far stall still dusted with glitter from Hippy Girl's hoops.

Trucker and I wait in silence. No one has joined the line behind us. It's an odd gap in the collective need to pee. Perhaps I'm channeling it all, perhaps all their urination impulses are funneling through my body because suddenly I *really* need to pee.

Kegels help, but nothing beats external pressure. Kids are shameless experts at this, but they can get away with grabbing their crotches in public in a way that adults never can. I'm convinced that with baggy enough jeans, no one can tell when you dig hands deep into pockets, sneaking fingertips over to crotch in order to provide that direct urethral pressure. Cynthia tells me I'm crazy to think no one can see what I'm doing, but sometimes I have no choice.

I lean around Trucker just to double-check the stall status. The suburbans are struggling to pull the far stall door shut while Bettie is still ensconced in the near one. The door of the middle stall is ajar.

"I think that one might be free." I point urgently with my elbow, fearful of loosing the pressure of the pee-tourniquet I've applied.

Trucker walks forward to check, pulls the door open, and immediately recoils.

"With good reason!" he says, returning to the short line

where I'm now hopping from one foot to the other. I might as well be a three-year-old.

Bettie reemerges and goes back to the mirrors. I have a strong sense of déjà vu.

"Femmes…" Trucker grunts impatiently.

I must look like I am about to burst because Trucker gestures magnanimously. "You first," he says with a slight bow.

Never one to look a gift horse—or gift trucker—in the mouth, I nod my gratitude and move toward the stall. My tiny, rapid steps are a feeble attempt to walk while still keeping my thighs pressed tight together. I can tell this is going to be close. I'm unbuckling my belt with one hand as I swing the stall door open with the other.

"It must be Noah's Ark day today," I hear Betty say with amusement. Then she sings, "The animals went in two by two, two by two…"

With my internal waters rising, my brain can't quite process her words. I struggle to drop trou, bend forward, swing butt over seat and reach out to close the stall door, all in one deft complex of choreography. Only when my outstretched hand hits soft belly do I finally understand: Trucker has slipped into the stall right behind me.

He closes the door and leans back against it, folding his arms across his flattened chest.

"Uh?" I grab for the waistband of my pants and try to stand. My pants are already at mid-thigh, ready to provide a sanitary cushion between my body and the less than pristine toilet seat. Even as I clench the muscles of my pelvic floor, I know that my bladder is way ahead of the rest of me, already breathing its own sigh of relief as it releases. We have passed the peeing point of no return.

"Might as well just let it go," he coaches.

I hover above the toilet for just a moment longer before finally giving in.

"Ah!" I sigh as I feel my bladder ache and collapse, muscles bearing down to force a hard stream of warm liquid. It seems to go on forever. An entire park's worth of pee. Over my splashing sound I hear the suburban girls two doors down.

"Don't fight it," the slightly more sober one says. "You'll feel better after."

"But I don't want to," the other laments. "It's so gross!"

I can hear her swallowing hard, fighting a losing battle but not yet willing to concede.

"I promise I'll hold your hair back."

A deep sigh and a burp in response.

I sigh too, my channeled flow having finally come to an end. I've never been a "tinkler," letting urine dribble out of me as if almost by accident, and I certainly am not going to be one now as he watches. I am a binary pee-er: on or off, one hundred percent committed until the last drop. Having reached full stop, I twist to the right and tease at the underside of the dispenser searching for toilet paper. Nothing. I peer through the translucent plastic, seeing only an empty cardboard core.

"Damn!" I mutter.

"Guess you'll just have to drip dry," Trucker shrugs.

It is one thing to succumb to the uncontrollable need to pee while being watched. It is an entirely different matter to simply sit with an audience and wait to dry.

"Slide back," he says, reaching for his heavy Caterpillar belt buckle. "I need to pee too."

I'm confused. I start to stand but he makes eye contact, raising one eyebrow in a dare. The energy of his body's forward movement pushes me back down.

"Slide your pants to your ankles, move back and spread your knees." His voice is quiet but firm.

He unzips his fly. The heavy belt pulls the corners of his pants down and out of the way. He reaches into his plaid boxers to expose one of those stand-to-pee packers I've heard about.

Realistic and functional. Who knew?

"Don't worry, I'm very accurate with this," he encourages.

"I sure hope so," I mumble.

With little room to maneuver, I slide back until my spine hits the large metal pipe joint where water inflow meets flushing lever. It digs in just under my ribs. I look down at the narrow space between my legs and widen it, pushing my legs as far apart as the grimy porcelain will allow.

Trucker steps in closer and aims. I can see the hem of his white tank draping lazily over his guide hand. I hold my breath and then watch in amazement as a narrow stream of yellow arches downward between my legs.

"Wow!" I exclaim nervously. I can feel the heat pass close, like a molten lava waterfall, but my naked thighs stay dry. "You really are precise," I concede, closing my eyes and trying to stay perfectly still.

I hear a moan from the far stall. It still isn't clear if the suburban teen will win or lose her regurgitation fight.

By the sound of it, Bettie is still primping at the mirrors. Her singing is more animated now: Paulina Rubio's "Boys will be boys, they like to play around..."

There is something in the chestnut roughness of her voice that strikes like a match against the center strip of my belly, igniting a new awareness in my crotch.

I open my eyes. Trucker is still peeing a steady stream. I follow the coursing liquid upstream, past the dirty nails tensioning his precision instrument, past the thick belly pressing out into the stained shirt, all the way up to Trucker's tucked chin. Without moving his head, he lifts his eyes to mine and cracks a crooked smile.

"Impressive, eh? Let me show you just how *precise* I can really be."

I cock my head, unsure of his meaning. I've lost track of the larger question of how I came to be sitting here with a total stranger peeing between my legs. For now, I am focused on the more specific one at hand.

"Precise?"

His answer comes not in words but in a change in the microclimate at my crotch. I feel the heat, the rise in humidity, the building of an on-shore breeze first. It is like one of those disturbing San Francisco days when the wind reverses, coming from the northeast, bringing the Central Valley heat to the Bay and, with it, an uneasy feeling that the world could combust at any moment.

And it does...when his pee hits directly, accurately, purpose-fully onto the head of my clit.

"Fuck," I grunt, trying not to move and unable to hold still.

Outside, Bettie's singing has switched from lyrics to a warm hum.

I look up at Trucker. He is completely absorbed and focused, the tip of his tongue poking out between his firm lips. He coaxes the line of pee up and down the shaft of my clit as softly and gently as if it were the tip of his tongue.

The pee splatters against the opening of my front hole, runs down across the bridge of my perineum and splashes across my ass. Flashbacks to childhood baths, legs splayed up along the hard, cold tile as I fought to position the faucet's flow directly onto my clit.

"Jesus!" I gasp, my jaw dropping open as the energy pours down through by body, drawn down by the eddy of pee sweeping across my cunt, washing it all clean.

"I don't think I can fight it anymore!" I hear the suburban girl say from the far stall. A loud audible hiccup follows.

"Come as you are, as you were, as I want you to be..." Betty croons Nirvana without a hint of irony.

I bite into my lip. He is still peeing and the flow is even more targeted, moving slowly back up, stalking the head of my clit again. I know that when he reaches it, I will come. He's moving closer, past the vaginal opening, up across my own urethra, up to where my inner lips curve inward, giving him cover before the last pounce. He is teasing at the base of my clit, continuing up, up, up...I arch back and feel the orgasm gather in my belly.

Dry heaves echo from the far stall.

"Don't worry, I've got your hair. Just let it out..."

The sound of full-on retching.

I think I hear Bettie's fingers making what I can only describe as a golf clap.

I'm so close now, just two beats from my own kind of release...when it stops.

Everything stops.

The heat, the moisture, the sound all stop, flowing down and away in an instant.

"What the fuck?" I cock my head and crack open one eye.

Trucker is smirking, his dick still in his hand. "Sorry, sometimes you run dry at just the most inopportune moments."

My disappointment is clear. Without shifting the pre-come arch of my body, I scan my eyes slowly down to his dick and frown.

"Air drying," he says, as if in answer to my unspoken question.

I focus in on his taupe member. A single drop of golden urine dangles heavily from the tip. Slowly, I use my heels for leverage to pull myself along the toilet seat. Perched on the front edge, I lean forward and, with the tip of my tongue, off-load the droplet into my mouth. I pause to suckle on just the tip of his cock, wrapping my lips around only this side of its equator, its full roundness like a Tootsie pop in my mouth. My upper lip presses back against my own nasal septum and I feel satiated.

I stand, pants dropping down around my ankles, and press my belly into his, pushing him back against the stall door. I can feel his hand at his cock, trapped between us, the shaft pressing down into my crotch. I push my lips hard against his, feeling the firm jaw and sprouting whiskers at his chin. I force my tongue between his teeth, moving the taste of urine into his mouth like the passing of a hard candy between us.

With a sucking sound, I pull back.

"I've been told that if you're marooned on a desert island, you can drink your own urine to survive."

"Yum..." he replies.

I reach down and pull up my pants. I fasten my belt as he does the same. It is crowded now in the stall with us both standing. He tries to turn, starting to navigate our exit, but I push him back once more against the door. I grab at his crotch, holding it firmly in one hand. He does the same to mine and our eyes lock.

"Thanks," I say. "I needed that."

We both give one hard squeeze, as if shaking hands, then break contact. With a few more contortions, we find our way out of the stall.

Bettie catches my eye in the mirror. "Thanks, fellas. I needed that too." She smacks her red lips, perfecting the long-finished application of lipstick, and gathers her things.

I nod and smile back.

"What took you so long?" Cynthia queries as I plop down on the grass beside her. "I was beginning to get bored. Plus it's starting to get cold." She shivers, her long fleece no match for the cool, foggy breeze rolling through the park.

"Sorry. There was a line. You know how the bathrooms can be kind of crowded here."

"Now where was I?"

I watch as she tries to remember where we'd left off our conversation, stretching my legs to adjust into the not-quite-air-dried dampness in my jeans.

"Someplace interesting, I'm sure." I smile, not needing to care quite as much as before.

# TWO DOMS FOR DINNER

by Dorothy Freed

"Do you remember the fantasy you whispered in my ear one night in the playroom?" Sir inquires. "The one where you're made to serve two dominant men—in every way?"

"Two…dominant men, Sir," I say. My voice goes up a notch on the word *two*. "And in every way? Did I say that?"

"You did, D, and I've arranged it," he says, grinning. "My old friend Charles is coming to dinner tomorrow evening. You remember him, don't you?"

"How could I not? You lent me to him at a party once or twice, years ago. Had quite a way with a whip, didn't he?" I'm blushing as I speak, and my lady parts clench at the memory.

"Still my little slut, even at your age," he replies proudly. "Wear something hot, with stockings and a garter belt underneath, no bra or panties."

"Yes, Sir," I say.

Sir and I have been a Dominant/submissive couple for many years. And although the sex is less frequent and our play is less strenuous than it once was, we're lucky enough to still be in love and happy with the lifestyle we've chosen. Still, it's been years since we were active in the BDSM party scene, and I miss the thrill of play with other Doms—under Sir's watchful eye.

On the day of Charles's visit I'm so excited I can hardly speak, imagining the evening to come. I spend hours choosing an outfit, finally fixing on a clingy, low-cut, burgundy-colored top that barely covers the fullness of my breasts; a flouncy, knee-length black skirt that makes me feel girlish; and the comfortable, low-heeled slippers my feet insist on these days—and no bra or panties, as ordered.

After I'm finally dressed, I apply makeup and fuss with my short, silvery hair, then check my appearance in our full-length bedroom mirror. *Not bad*, I think, smiling at my image and enjoying the low hum of desire between my legs.

I glance at the clock. It's a little after five. Our guest is expected to arrive at six thirty. I go into the kitchen, set the table and assemble the ingredients for a simple meal: pasta and veggies with Sir's favorite marinara sauce, a simple salad with walnut oil and wine vinegar dressing, crusty bread and butter, and ice cream for dessert. Keeping it simple will leave more time for play.

I've set water on to boil for the pasta and I'm standing at the stove stirring my sauce when Sir comes up behind me. "You make one hell of a beautiful kitchen slave, D," he says as I feel his warm hands cupping my breasts and his fingers lightly tweaking my nipples. I arch my back and sigh with pleasure. "Martha Stewart of the BDSM set," I say, happily. "That's me."

"And now for the finishing touch to your outfit," Sir says, slipping my black chain-link collar around my neck. "There, that's my girl."

Charles arrives on the dot of six thirty, a tall, thick-bodied man in his early sixties, with a box of dark chocolates in his hand as a gift for his hostess. His hair's a bit thinner and grayer than I remember it. He's put on some weight as well. But his full lips are soft on mine when he kisses me, and I melt into him as his tongue explores my mouth. I'm flushed with arousal when he releases me. "D, you look beautiful," he says.

"Thank you, Sir," I say, accepting his gift. I take his coat and hang it up in the study while he exchanges hearty handshakes with my owner. "You're one lucky man to have a woman like that," I hear him tell Sir, and so the evening begins.

The men sit at either end of the table, chatting with each other while watching every move I make. I serve the dinner as gracefully as possible. But the truth is I'm so excited that I'm stammering. Sir slides a hand up my skirt and teases my pussy lips when I set his plate on the table. "No panties," he informs Charles, who waves me over to his end of the table to confirm this. I look down, blushing as he fondles me, but I'm grinning like a fool.

Neither man drinks wine while they're topping, but I pour myself a glass when I finally sit down. I'm told dinner is delicious but I'm too aroused to taste a thing. When the dishes are cleared, I serve the ice cream, accompanied by the chocolates. There's a tension building between the three of us by the time the meal is over, and I clear the table and carry the dishes to the sink. My pulse quickens as both men watch me with predatory smiles.

"Use the bathroom if you need to, D, and then go straight to the playroom and undress. I want to find you kneeling face down and ass up when we join you. I placed a pillow on the floor to spare your knees because I'm a very kind man."

"Yes, Sir, thank you, Sir," I mumble. I feel them watching me as I head down the hall.

I enter the playroom and undress, then kneel as ordered, and wait, heart pounding, clit pulsing in anticipation of what is to come. The warm air that blows from the room's heating vent feels cool against my naked skin. In spite of my excitement, I'm shifting my weight, hoping they'll get here before my knees give out. I hear heavy footsteps coming toward me, then enter the room, and the men stand gazing down at me.

"Well isn't this a sight to behold," Sir says, reaching down to tease the crack of my ass. I arch my back slightly and sigh with pleasure. By now my legs begin trembling and I'm ordered to rise and present myself—legs apart, shoulders back, hands behind my head. I stand proud, smiling, knowing the pose makes my breasts stand out. Charles is eating me up with his eyes.

Sir cuffs my wrists and attaches them to chains that hang from the ceiling.

"I've laid out some of my favorite toys," he tells Charles, indicating the various implements of pleasure spread out on his desk. "I'm going to give D a warm-up with some of these toys and show you how she responds to them. Feel free to join in. The more the merrier."

He begins with the small rubber whip, which is actually my favorite, dangling it over my breasts, whipping them lightly and making my nipples even harder than they already are. Behind me Charles's big, warm hands slide down over my back and rear before delivering a series of smacks to my asscheeks.

The two Doms switch positions. Sir moves behind me, spanking me with the long-handled leather paddle, which makes a loud slapping sound as it strikes. Charles, facing my front, gazes into my eyes as he tweaks my nipples and then amuses himself by lightly slapping my breasts, making them swing back and forth.

"Ohhh, Sirs," I moan, as the sensations intensify.

"She responds well to nipple clamps. Try the small red ones," Sir suggests.

"Excellent idea, don't mind if I do." With an evil grin Charles clips each of my nipples, teasing them with his fingers. My breasts begin to tingle; they feel lit up from the inside out.

"Try this larger one on her pussy and clip her lips together,"

Sir says. "You'll get quite a rise out of her that way." I yelp as he applies it. "And here, hang this weight from it." He hands Charles one. I yelp again as it's attached, and I feel the weight of it swinging between my legs.

Both Doms step back to admire their work. "Let's try something different," Sir says, and disconnects me from the chains. "Would you care for a blow job?" he inquires politely.

"Well, yes, just to be polite," Charles is grinning from ear to ear.

"Don't I get a say in this?" I wonder aloud, teasing.

"Of course not," Sir says. "Get down on your knees, woman. Ask Charles if you may have his permission to give him a blow job."

"May I please have your permission to give you a blow job, Sir?" I ask Charles, kneeling before him. My voice is a whisper and my face flames with embarrassment.

"Yes, of course, my dear, since you've asked so respectfully." As Charles says this, he unzips his fly, freeing his cock from his pants.

It's half hard and growing rapidly, with a mushroom shaped head and a thick, veiny shaft. I reach for it, feeling it grow in my hands. I inhale its musky fragrance, licking at the salty drops of precome that form at its tip. Unhinging my jaw, I draw the full length of it into my mouth, feeling it press against the back of my throat. Charles sighs deeply with pleasure, clasps his hands behind my head, holding it in position, and begins pumping his hips.

"Good at it, isn't she," Sir comments.

"Oh god, yes," Charles says, moaning. "Can she do this all night?"

"Probably," my owner replies. "Shall we find out?"

I'm aware of Sir watching me. *I'm making him proud*, I think, and although my jaw begins aching, I keep on, desiring only to please.

"I'm getting ready to come," Charles says urgently, pulling out. Wrapping my hands around his cock, I stroke him to orgasm. His thick white come sprays out over my breasts. I look up at Sir beseechingly, my pussy clenching, longing to be fucked.

"You've earned it, D," Sir says, understanding my need. He bends me over his desk, while Charles settles himself comfortably in Sir's computer chair to watch the action. I squeal when the weighted clips are removed from my pussy lips and moan as he enters me, fucking me hard. Reaching down, I rub my clit with my fingers. I'm so turned on I come almost immediately. The orgasm is powerful and goes on for a long time. Sir comes with a groan and bends over me, nuzzling my neck and stroking my hair.

"Bravo, my friends," Charles says, with a big wide smile. "Good show."

We tidy up and move to the living room, where I serve the men wine and the rest of the chocolates. They sit on the couch chatting, caressing me affectionately while I sit at their feet.

"Tonight has been fun," Sir tells Charles. "Let's do this again soon."

"Just let me know when," Charles replies. He reaches down to cup my breasts in his hands. "It'll be my pleasure."

"Mine too, Sirs," I say, grinning.

The evening with two Doms is a success beyond my dreams.

# THE ASSISTANT

## by Tiffany Reisz

"What would you say to a three-day weekend?" Lennon asked, and Ivy could have rung his beautiful neck for even suggesting such a thing.

"Why?" she asked, turning from the filing cabinet in his private office to face him. She'd been digging for something she hadn't actually needed, which she did about five times a day simply to have an excuse to go into Lennon's office.

"Why? You don't say 'Why?' when your boss offers you a three-day weekend. You say 'Hell yes, boss. Best idea I've ever heard.'"

Ivy pursed her lips at him. "Why?" she asked again.

"You and I both worked all weekend last weekend," Lennon said, leaning back in his vintage leather swivel chair. He put his hands behind his head and raised his eyebrows, waiting for her to contradict him. Ivy envied the hands on his hair. Lennon was a young silver fox, and didn't seem to mind at all that he was mid-thirties and already mostly gray.

"No big deal." She waved her hand and sat in the club chair

across from his desk. When she crossed her legs, she watched him, hoping he'd look at her legs. He did for a split second before meeting her eyes again. "It's not like you didn't pay me overtime." And it's not like she hadn't loved every second of it. Weekend work meant Lennon out of a suit and in jeans and his favorite ratty concert T-shirts. Saturday had been Pink Floyd. Sunday belonged to Eminem.

Lennon leaned forward, rested his elbows on his desk and looked her in the eyes. Blue eyes, bright but tired.

"Katie broke up with me," he said.

"What? Why?" Breaking up with Lennon seemed as insane as setting a Rembrandt on fire. Who did that?

"This is awkward." Lennon wrinkled his face up, and it was as handsome wincing as it was smiling.

"Me?" Ivy asked.

"She said I spent more time with my assistant than I do with her."

"You do."

"If you weren't, you know, you, it wouldn't be a problem. But you are you and that's a problem. For her, not me."

"Did you just tell me I'm pretty?"

Lennon glared at her. "You know you are. Katie wouldn't care about that if I didn't spend my weeks with you *and* my weekends with you. She says you're my work wife."

*Then make me your real wife, you beautiful idiot.*

"So why the three-day weekend? You trying to get rid of me?" Ivy asked.

"Never," he said vehemently, and she cherished that vehemence. "Jack's taking me out tomorrow for a recovery day of hiking and drinking. Then he's forcing me entirely against my will to go to a party at a friend's house Saturday night. And if I'm not here, there's no reason for you to be here."

"Three-day weekend it is then." Ivy stood up and smoothed her skirt down. "And thank you. I got invited to a party too this weekend," she said, a lie. It wasn't a party so much as brunch with her sister. "Maybe it's the same party as yours."

Lennon stood up and walked around his desk. Gently he lifted the little gold Star of David pendant she wore on a necklace. His fingers were so light on her skin she felt goosebumps all over her arms. And Lennon stood so close she could smell his light cologne.

"No offense, but I don't think you go to the same parties Jack and I go to. Although if you want to come with us, you can. Beautiful women are always welcome at that house." He said it like a dare, like a challenge.

"Is it one of *those* parties?" Ivy asked as Lennon played with the six corners of the star. They were as comfortable with each other as people who worked in close quarters had to be. She'd smack his hand when he reached for her food. He'd let her sleep on his shoulder when they took red-eye flights to London. But this little moment felt different, felt personal.

"One of those parties, yeah..." He looked a little embarrassed and she adored him for it. He'd been careful to keep his personal life separate from his professional life, even with her. But one Sunday afternoon she'd had to run to his apartment for reasons entirely work-related, and while he'd been on the phone in the other room, she'd glanced through a half-open door and seen Lennon's bedroom. A leather flogger sat on the pillow and handcuffs dangled from the headboard. When Lennon had caught her looking he'd blushed and stammered an apology. She'd told him she didn't care as long as what he was doing in his free time was consensual. It had been the first thing she'd thought of to say and only later had she realized it made her sound boring, virginal and utterly vanilla. What she'd wanted to say was, "*The handcuffs? The flogger? Lennon, that's nothing to apologize for. It's sexy as hell, and I volunteer as your next victim.*" There hadn't been a night since she hadn't fallen asleep dreaming of his body, that bed, and those handcuffs on her wrists while she made herself come.

Ivy wrapped her hand around his fingers holding her pendant.

"Lenn—"

Lennon let the pendant go like it had burned him.

"You work for me," he said.

"I know. I know." She raised her hands in surrender.

She knew. She knew. They'd had this discussion once before on a night flight when neither of them could sleep but seemingly the rest of the plane could. He'd admitted his attraction to her, and she to him, and the only thing that had stopped them from joining the mile-high club had been Lennon's innate sense of decency that kept him from sleeping with an employee ten years his junior. She knew if she made the first move it would happen. But she just couldn't bring herself to do it.

Lennon took a step back. She stopped herself from taking a step forward. "Have a good three-day weekend. I'll see you on Monday."

Ivy smiled. "Monday."

Then she took her file, walked out of his office, and sat at her desk. She didn't trust herself to walk back into Lennon's office without declaring her love and/or lust for him, so instead she opened their messenger app and typed, "Need car service for the party? Where? When?"

Lennon wrote back thirty seconds later. "Yes, please. Saturday, nine. 152 Riverside Drive. Warn the driver we'll be dressed weird."

"How weird?" she typed back.

"*Eyes Wide Shut* weird."

"I'll make a note in the comment field."

And that's when it hit Ivy...she knew where the party was. She knew when it was. She knew she could go to it if she wanted to go to it.

She wanted to go to it.

Lennon had said *"Eyes Wide Shut* weird" and implied he'd be dressed in some sort of costume. That would make it much easier to slip in and out. She didn't want to do anything but see him, and be part of his world for a little while. She wouldn't even talk to him. But to pass unobserved she'd have to dress the part herself. Saturday morning she made an appointment with her stylist who did her hair in a complicated and very un-Ivy updo. She bought a slinky white dress and a white masquerade mask. Lennon had never seen her wear her hair like this. He'd never seen her wear white. And with the mask covering half her face, he'd have no idea it was her. Since it was one of "those" parties, Ivy also invested in a pair of white seamed stockings and a garter belt and white high heels with white ribbons that tied at the ankle. Once dressed she looked the opposite of her usual work self. Her own mother wouldn't recognize her.

When nine o'clock rolled around, she grabbed a cab. On her way there she told herself that if the party wasn't her scene, all she had to do was turn around and leave. She could do this. Get in, get out, don't cause trouble. Don't reveal herself and whatever she did, no contact with Lennon. None.

The cab dropped her off, and she paid her driver. It took her a couple seconds to work up the courage to step out and climb the stairs of the black-and-white three-story townhouse. Through the door she could hear the sounds of music and laughter and the usual party revelry going on inside. Before she knocked she tried the knob and found the door unlocked. As quickly and quietly as she could, Ivy stepped inside.

Oh.

Oh...

Oh, no.

Lennon hadn't been exaggerating. It really was one of *those* kinds of parties.

Everywhere she looked she saw couples coupling. Kissing in doorways, draped over each other on sofas and in the room to the left, some sort of sitting room, she saw a woman kneeling on her hands and knees on a coffee table while a man in a dark three-piece suit and devil horns fucked her from behind. They weren't alone in the room, not at all. People stood around watching, cheering. Someone even held a stopwatch in his hand. Cash was scattered on the table around the woman's hands and knees. From what Ivy could tell it was a contest and The Devil was contestant number two. The previous contestant had fucked the woman twelve minutes and sixteen seconds before coming. The current contestant just fucked his way past the ten minute mark. Someone in the crowd said they were neck in neck. Someone else said they were cock in cock.

Ivy stared, mesmerized by the scene. It was porn—beautiful, erotic, playful live porn—and she couldn't look away. Her nipples tightened under her low-cut dress and her pussy swelled at the sight of the woman taking the cock so casually in a room of a dozen people. Ivy flushed and felt herself growing wet, and her vagina clenched at nothing, wanting something inside it.

"Want to play?" came an accented voice from behind her. She turned and saw the man who'd spoken. He wore a military-style long coat, white shirt open at the collar, plus breeches and Hessian boots polished to a high shine. He was impossibly handsome, with shoulder-length, dark, wavy hair and a wolfish gleam in his dark eyes.

"I...no. Just watching," she said.

"I shouldn't play anyway," he said with a dramatic sigh. "I always win. Hardly fair, is it?" He lifted her hand to his lips at if to kiss the back of it. Instead he flipped her hand over and pressed his lips to the center of her palm. With a wink he walked away, no doubt seeking out more amenable prey.

Ivy turned to leave and came face to bare chest with a man wearing nothing but leather pants. Nothing. Not even shoes. He had shaggy hair, brown skin and a wicked smile. She felt a sudden pang of attraction to him.

"Oh, sorry," she said. "I—"

"You must be new," he said, narrowing his eyes at her.

"I'm very new. Very, very new."

"We like newbies around here." He cupped her chin. "Tell me what you want, and I'll make sure you get it."

Ivy opened her mouth, closed it, then saw Lennon striding down the hallway toward the front door. He wasn't dressed nearly as oddly as everyone else at the party. He had on black trousers, a black vest, and a white shirt with the cuffs rolled to his elbows. His only nod to the party atmosphere was the black mask he wore over his eyes. Impossible not to know it was him, however. Not with that smile and that salt-and-pepper hair.

"Him," Ivy whispered. "I want him."

"You sure about that?" the man in the leather pants asked. She couldn't believe she'd spoken her wish aloud.

"I am."

"Then kiss me."

She kissed him and found his mouth warm and his lips skillful. She'd been so busy with work for Lennon she hadn't gone on a date in six months. Whoever this man was, she didn't know, but she also didn't care. He had big hands that felt good on her waist, and a girl needed kissing sometimes. Even by a stranger.

And then Ivy was off her feet. Entirely, completely and totally off her feet, being carried over the man's shoulder.

"Oh my God," she said, and the man heard her.

"I'm a firefighter in real life," he said, slapping her on the ass. "Trust me, I know what I'm doing."

"Glad one of us does."

"Come on, man," he said as he carried her into a room. "I caught something for you."

"Aw, you shouldn't have, Jack." Ivy recognized Lennon's voice.

"You've had a hard week. You've earned some fun."

So this was Jack, Lennon's kinky friend who dragged him to parties? Is this something they did together? Share women? Ivy wanted to be jealous if it was, but instead she found the prospect arousing, the thought of being passed back and forth between them.

Ivy gripped the sofa cushion hard and tried to get her bearings. She was in a room, a very nice but small room with antique furniture like out of *Pride and Prejudice* or something. Door closed. No lights on but for the fire burning in the fireplace. No bed. Fireplace with an ornate, dark-wood mantel and a low fire burning. Other than the couch she and Jack sat on, there was one armchair across from them and a huge steamer trunk that acted as a coffee table. Lennon sat in the chair and held his wine glass lightly between his fingertips. He was watching her.

"This is how it works," Jack was saying as he slowly eased her panties down her legs. "Since you're new...I do whatever I want to do to you and you say 'Red' when and if you want me to stop. And what I want to do to you is fuck you while my friend watches. Then he will do whatever he wants to do to you. He won't be nearly as gentle with you as I will. Yes? No? Red?"

Ivy glanced at Lennon, who grinned at Jack's warning.

She was scared, her heart pounding, her blood pumping so hard in her ears it sounded like the roar of an ocean.

"Yes."

She whispered the word so Lennon couldn't recognize her voice. But Jack heard.

"Good answer," he said, and casually unzipped his pants to pull out his cock.

He reached for a condom from the bowl of them on the steamer trunk. She couldn't believe this was happening as he stroked himself to his full hardness and rolled on the condom so matter-of-factly he could have been tying his shoes if he'd been wearing any.

"You can say 'Red' anytime," Lennon said from his armchair.

"We're big boys. We have self-control."

Ivy nodded her understanding, taking comfort in his words. It made it easier when Jack pushed her legs wide open. Out of the corner of her eye she could see Lennon leaning forward, lifting his chin to see her better. Since she'd gotten a full wax yesterday, she knew he could see everything—her open labia, her clitoris, her wetness—and it aroused her even more to know Lennon was seeing her body without even knowing it was hers. Jack inserted his index finger into her and rubbed along the walls of her vagina.

"New and eager," Jack said with a dirty grin, clearly impressed by how wet she was. She realized quickly he wasn't talking to her, but Lennon. "I'll open her up for you. You finish her off. Sound like a plan?"

Lennon answered, "A perfect plan."

Jack gripped her by the back of the knees and knelt between her thighs. This was happening…it was actually happening…Ivy breathed quick, shallow breaths to calm herself. It didn't work. Jack had his cock in his hand, and the tip pushed against her clitoris. A spasm of pleasure shot through her, and Ivy instinctively lifted her hips to offer herself to him. With one smooth stroke he was inside her. He pushed her dress up to her stomach, gripped her waist and rode her with firm steady thrusts. She couldn't believe she was doing this, letting a strange man fuck her while her boss watched. She lifted her head and watched Jack's cock pumping in and out of her. No denying it—she was doing this. Her head fell back on the sofa and she turned toward Lennon. She didn't mean to meet his eyes but as soon as she did, she couldn't look away. *See me…*she wanted to say to him. *Look at me. I'm not who you think I am. I'm not just your assistant. I'm a woman, and I need you like this…* He saw her. Those blue eyes of his never left hers as Jack fucked her. If only he knew her, knew it was her. *It's me…*she told him with her eyes. *It's Ivy, and I want you enough I did this for you, to be with you…*

Jack was fucking her hard now, and Ivy opened her legs wider for him. Lennon moved from the chair and sat on the steamer trunk next to them. She wasn't ready for him to touch her, but touch her he did, pressing his hand onto her lower stomach and pushing down as if trying to feel Jack's cock moving inside her. Then Lennon dipped his fingertips into his white wine and touched her clitoris with them. She inhaled sharply, nearly flinching at the sudden coolness on her burning body. He grinned as he rubbed the swollen knot of flesh, toying with it at first before giving it the serious attention it needed. Her hips moved in tight circles as Lennon touched her and Jack fucked her. All sensation was concentrated in her pelvis, in her sex. Lennon worked her clitoris with two fingers and it was more than she could take. This man she adored and lusted after touching her so intimately while she was being fucked…she came with a cry and a shudder, her hole gripping and grabbing at Jack's cock still pounding her. He slammed his orgasm into her as Ivy lay back, closed her eyes and took it.

She was empty inside again and her body felt warm and drowsy. Somewhere she heard a door open and close. Ivy was being lifted into strong arms. Limp and spent, she let the strong arms pull her upright and press her into the back of the couch. Thighs nudged her legs open and someone penetrated her again. Ivy opened her eyes and found herself in Lennon's arms, her chin on his shoulder, her legs wound around his waist, as he pinned her to the back of the couch with his cock inside her.

His hands were on her back, lowering the zipper on her dress. She stiffened, suddenly wide awake.

"We're alone," Lennon said, kissing her bare shoulder as he slid the straps of her dress down her arms. Down, down it went until he'd pushed her dress to her waist, baring her breasts for him. "Don't be shy."

Shy? She was finally having sex with the man she'd adored for two years. Ivy leaned back, arching for him, offering her breasts to him. He ran his hands over them, squeezing them lightly, holding them in his palms as he licked and sucked her nipples. Lennon was sucking her nipples and it felt better than anything had ever felt in her life. Fucking her softly at first, deeply, and then harder and harder. Jack had warned her Lennon would be rougher with her than he was. But Jack hadn't warned her it would feel this good. He was fucking her so hard now she could feel it in her stomach. She loved it, needed it, had needed it ever since she went to work for Lennon. He pulled out of her but only to turn her, bending her over the sofa arm. He entered her from behind and fucked her deep, his hands holding her breasts and squeezing them, tugging the nipples until she moaned.

"You like this?" he asked, and his voice sounded so unlike him. So forceful and dominant.

"Yes."

"When I'm done fucking you I'm going to flog you. Then fuck you again. You want that?"

"Yes." She was so wet from his thrusts she felt it dripping down her thighs.

"I knew you would."

But how did he know? He didn't even know it was her.

He didn't know...

"Red," Ivy said.

Lennon pulled out of her immediately as Ivy yanked her dress back up.

"What's wrong?" he asked, looking scared, concerned. He touched her arm. "I didn't hurt you, did I?"

"No," she said, scrambling off the sofa. "I'm sorry."

He reached for her again as she headed for the door, but she kept walking away from him and out of the house.

What was she thinking, having sex with her own boss without telling him it was her? Jack knew he was having anonymous sex with a girl he'd never met before. But Lennon didn't, and that wasn't right. No matter how much she wanted him, how good it felt, it wasn't right.

By Monday morning, Ivy had pulled herself together as best as she could. She dressed in her normal clothes, did her hair the normal way, prepared to act as normally as she could. She wouldn't blow her cover. She wouldn't confess. She wouldn't put Lennon in a horribly awkward position because she'd followed him to his party like some lovesick puppy. She would be a grown-up and carry the secret. In the break room she poured two cups of coffee and marched into his office like it was any other day.

"Morning," she said, handing him his coffee.

"How was your weekend?"

"Good. Yours?" Ivy asked, keeping her face empty of expression.

"Good. Too short."

"Typical, right?"

"Right. But back to work. Can you bring me the Close Brothers file?"

She walked to the filing cabinet and opened the top drawer. When she pulled out the file, something fell out onto the floor.

Ivy bent to pick it up and found a black mask in her hand.

She looked at it, then looked at Lennon, who was smiling smugly at her with his hands clasped behind his head.

"You tan easily, you know," he said. "But your Star of David pendant blocks the sun. You have a six-pointed pale spot on your chest."

"You knew it was me?"

"The whole time..."

"I didn't mean to. Jack was there and he asked me what I wanted and I said you. What's going to happen?" Ivy's heart pounded outside her chest, the mask clutched in her hand, memories of his mouth on her breasts and his fingers on her clitoris setting her to blushing and flushing and burning inside and out.

Lennon stood up and walked over to her. As he passed the door, he closed it and locked it.

"What would you say to a four-day weekend?" he asked. Before she could answer he dipped his head and kissed her slow and deep and long, his tongue touching hers, his hands on her lower back and roaming lower, and his hips pushing into hers. She pulled back from the kiss and stared up at him. He knew. And she knew. And they'd done it anyway. And now they were going to do it again.

"I would say... Hell yes, boss. Best idea I've ever heard."

# ABOUT THE AUTHORS

**L. MARIE ADELINE** is the pseudonym for Lisa Gabriele, a best-selling author and award-winning TV producer. Her S.E.C.R.E.T. erotica trilogy was published in more than thirty countries. She lives in Toronto.

**VALERIE ALEXANDER** lives in Los Angeles. Her work has been published in *Best of Best Women's Erotica, The Mammoth Book of Erotica, Best Bondage Erotica* and other anthologies.

**TARA BETTS** is the author of the poetry collection *Arc & Hue*. Tara's writing has also appeared in several journals and anthologies, including *Best Black Women's Erotica 2* and *Erotic Haiku*.

**AMY BUTCHER** is a writer, illustrator and silver-fox "liminal guide" who enjoys leading people through transformations. She is Chief Whimsy Officer of the erotic collaborative *Body Trust*, co-edited the 2015 IPPY Gold Medal-winning anthology *Sex Still Spoken Here* and authored the 2012 award-winning mystery novel *Paws for Consideration*.

**ROSE CARAWAY** is a writer, editor, narrator, audiobook producer and podcaster for the hit show "The Kiss Me Quick's" Erotica Podcast. She freely celebrates all things erotica with her wonderful Lurid Listeners, and is fondly known as "The Sexy Librarian" who scours the globe searching for sexy stories.

**DEBORAH CASTELLANO** (http://www.deborahmcastellano. com) made her erotica debut with "Courting Him" in *Best Women's Erotica 2009*. Her work includes "Party Girl" and "How to Become a Lady Adventurer" published by Freya's Bower, "Maid for You" in *Best Lesbian Erotica 2012*, "Tails" in *Anything for You* and "Day Job" in *Slave Girls*.

**HEIDI CHAMPA** is an extensively published author of erotic fiction. Find out more at heidichampa.blogpspot.com.

**DORIANA CHASE** lives in a seaside New England town with her husband and two cats. She writes and draws every day. Many of her short stories and articles have been published under different names, and she is currently working on two books: an erotic romance and a graphic novel. Visit her Facebook page at www.facebook.com/doriana.chase.

**ELIZABETH COLDWELL** lives and writes in London. Her stories have appeared in numerous anthologies, including five volumes of Best Women's Erotica. She can be found at The (Really) Naughty Corner, http://elizabethcoldwell.wordpress.com.

**J. CRICHTON** and **H. KEYES** both reside in Japan and have appeared in other erotica anthologies including *Can't Get Enough*, edited by Tenille Brown, and *Come Again: Sex Toy Erotica*, edited by Rachel Kramer Bussel.

**DOROTHY FREED** is the pseudonym of an erotica writer who lives near San Francisco. Her stories have appeared in anthologies including *Cheeky Spanking Stories, Twice the Pleasure, Ageless Erotica* and *Sex Still Spoken Here.* Her blog, *Sixty-Nine and Still Sexual,* is on her website, dorothyfreedwrites.com

**THEDA HUDSON**'s erotica presses sexual boundaries, boiling over with leather and latex, steaming with desire. Her work includes stories in *Best Lesbian Erotica 2011* and *2015*, *Best Lesbian Romance 2011* and *2012* and an urban paranormal novel, *Dyke Valiant.* She lives with four cats, one thousand books and one understanding partner.

**LAZULI JONES**'s particular brand of erotica has previously appeared in Torquere Press's *They Do* anthology and the *Mythologically Torqued* anthology. Her first novel, *Abyssal Zone,* is available from eXtasy Books. As a local performer and queer activist, Lazuli can be found haunting the stage in Ontario, Canada with an odd play or a bit of slam poetry.

**ELISE KING** is a former fiction editor and an MFA candidate, currently at work on her first novel. Her work has appeared in *Fine Lines.* She lives in Nebraska, and aside from her corporate day job, she spends every minute possible on her writing.

**ROSE P. LETHE** is a corporate copyeditor, copywriter and watcher of cat videos. After completing an MFA in creative writing, she found she could no longer stomach "serious literature," and has since turned to more enjoyable creative pursuits.

**TABITHA RAYNE** loves all things sensual, from painting nude ladies to writing erotic tales. Her erotic fantasy, *The Clockwork Butterfly Trilogy*, explores a dystopian future where sexual pleasure holds the key to survival. Her stories appear in anthologies from Cleis Press, Xcite, Ravenous Romance, Burning Books, Velvet Books and more.

**TIFFANY REISZ** is the author of the international bestselling Original Sinners series. Her book *The King* won the 2015 Lambda Award for Best Gay Erotica. Find her on Twitter @tiffanyreisz.

**RIA RESTREPO** has written just about everything from literary fiction to political humor under various names. Now she's focused on writing what she loves to read—mainly romance and erotica. Her erotic romance "Undercover Desires" was recently published in *Spy Games: Thrilling Spy Erotica* from House of Erotica books.

**D.R. SLATEN** began writing at a very young age. She spent most of her childhood with stories running in her head side by side with real stories in her life. Raising children, practicing law and life sidetracked her from her stories. Now her stories have revolted and found a way out.

**JESSICA TAYLOR** (jessicataylorwriter.com) is writing her first novel, an MMA erotic romance. You can read more of her work in *Spy Games: Thrilling Spy Erotica*. Jessica is the winner of a Texas Health Resources Literature and Medicine award and two Katey Lehman Awards for creative writing.

**JADE A. WATERS** (jadeawaters.com) once convinced a boyfriend that reading provocative synonyms from a thesaurus counted as foreplay, and she's been penning erotic tales in California ever since. Her short fiction appears in various anthologies including *Best Erotic Romance 2015*, *Best Women's Erotica 2014* and *Coming Together: Among the Stars*.

# ABOUT THE EDITOR

**RACHEL KRAMER BUSSEL** (rachelkramerbussel.com) is a New Jersey–based author, editor and blogger. She has edited over fifty books of erotica, including *Anything for You: Erotica for Kinky Couples; Best Bondage Erotica 2011, 2012, 2013, 2014* and *2015; The Big Book of Orgasms; Baby Got Back: Anal Erotica; Come Again: Sex Toy Erotica; Dirty Dates; Suite Encounters; Going Down; Irresistible; Gotta Have It; Obsessed; Women in Lust; Surrender; Orgasmic; Cheeky Spanking Stories; Bottoms Up; Spanked: Red-Cheeked Erotica; Fast Girls; Flying High; Do Not Disturb; Going Down; Tasting Him; Tasting Her; Please, Sir; Please, Ma'am; He's on Top; She's on Top; Caught Looking; Hide and Seek; Crossdressing;* and *Lust in Latex.* Her anthologies have won eight IPPY (Independent Publisher) Awards, and *Surrender* won the National Leather Association Samois Anthology Award. Her work has been published in over one hundred anthologies, including *Best American Erotica 2004* and *2006.* She wrote the popular "Lusty Lady" column for the *Village Voice.*

Rachel has written for *AVN, Bust,* cleansheets.com, *Cosmopolitan, Curve,* The Daily Beast, thefrisky.com, *Glamour,* Gothamist, *Harper's Bazaar,* Huffington Post, *Inked,* Mediabistro, *Newsday, New York Post, New York Observer, The New York Times, Penthouse,* The Root, Salon, *San Francisco Chronicle, Time Out New York, The Washington Post* and *Zink,* among others. She has appeared on *The Gayle King Show, The Martha Stewart Show, The Berman and Berman Show,* NY1 and Showtime's *Family Business.* She hosted the popular In the Flesh Erotic Reading Series, featuring readers from Susie Bright to Zane, and speaks at conferences, does readings and teaches erotic writing workshops across the country and online. She blogs at lustylady.blogspot.com and tweets @raquelita.